"You started  just that little bit nea_____der. "You *can't* stop n_____

Not breathing, Lila snatched the keys from behind him and jabbed him hard in the neck.

"What are you doing?" He was so surprised that he let her go.

Lila wasn't even thinking, she wasn't even feeling. She pushed open the door and staggered to the ground. She felt his arm reaching out for her, but she started swinging her bag at him. "Get away from me!" she screamed, her voice so shrill she couldn't believe it was hers. "Get away from me, I'm warning you."

She saw him freeze, suddenly frightened. "Calm down," he said, trying to sound as he usually did. "Get in the car, Lila, and I'll drive you home."

For one second, Lila almost believed she should get in the car and let John drive her home. But then she remembered his hands on her hair and the hardness of his voice just a few minutes before. "Don't you come near me!" she yelled. "Don't you ever come near me again!" With every ounce of strength she had, she took his car keys and threw them over the Point.

Bantam Books in the Sweet Valley High series
Ask your bookseller for the books you have missed

# DON'T GO HOME WITH JOHN

Written by
**Kate William**

Created by
**FRANCINE PASCAL**

BANTAM BOOKS
NEW YORK • TORONTO • LONDON • SYDNEY • AUCKLAND

RL 6, age 12 and up

DON'T GO HOME WITH JOHN
*A Bantam Book / January 1993*

Sweet Valley High is a registered trademark of Francine Pascal

Conceived by Francine Pascal

Produced by Daniel Weiss Associates, Inc.
33 West 17th Street
New York, NY 10011

Cover art by James Mathewuse

All rights reserved.
Copyright © 1992 by Francine Pascal.
Cover art copyright © 1992 by Daniel Weiss Associates, Inc.
No part of this book may be reproduced or transmitted
in any form or by any means, electronic or mechanical,
including photocopying, recording, or by any information
storage and retrieval system, without permission in
writing from the publisher.
For information address: Bantam Books.

If you purchased this book without a cover you should be aware
that this book is stolen property. It was reported as "unsold
and destroyed" to the publisher and neither the author nor the
publisher has received any payment for this "stripped book."

ISBN 0-553-29236-6

Published simultaneously in the United States and Canada

Bantam Books are published by Bantam Books, a division of Bantam
Doubleday Dell Publishing Group, Inc. Its trademark, consisting of the
words "Bantam Books" and the portrayal of a rooster, is Registered
in U.S. Patent and Trademark Office and in other countries. Marca
Registrada. Bantam Books, 666 Fifth Avenue, New York, New York
10103

PRINTED IN THE UNITED STATES OF AMERICA

OPM    0 9 8 7 6 5 4 3 2 1

# DON'T GO HOME WITH JOHN

# One

"I can't believe none of you have decided what you're wearing to my party yet," Lila Fowler said, shaking her head. "Not only is it a major social event, but it *is* just ten days away, you know."

Lila, Jessica Wakefield, Amy Sutton, Rosa Jameson, and Maria Santelli were having lunch in the Sweet Valley High cafeteria together on Wednesday afternoon. Two weeks ago Lila had announced that she was going to throw the biggest costume ball Sweet Valley had ever seen, and since then no one had been able to talk of anything else.

Jessica groaned. "Don't remind me. Sam and I have been arguing about our costumes for days. I want to go as a romantic couple, like Romeo

1

and Juliet. But you know Sam, all he's interested in is dirt-bike racing." She rolled her eyes. "He'll only go as Romeo and Juliet if they wear leather."

Marie laughed. "Count yourself lucky," she advised. "Winston's so romantic he wants to go as Tweedledum and Tweedledee."

Jessica couldn't help laughing. "Tweedledum and Tweedledee?"

Maria nodded. "You know what a great sense of humor Winston has," she said glumly. "He thinks it's funny."

Rosa rolled her beautiful brown eyes. "I don't know why you guys think you have problems," she said. "I haven't even decided who I'm going with yet, let alone what I'm going to wear."

"At least you have an excuse," Lila said. "You can't possibly choose a costume if you're still deciding on your date. But Amy has no excuse." She raised one perfect eyebrow in Amy's direction. "She's going with Barry."

Amy met Lila's raised eyebrow with one of her own. "I don't know what *you're* being so smug about," said Amy, pointing a carrot stick in her friend's direction. "I'll bet you don't know what you're going as yet, either."

Lila ran a slim hand through her light-brown hair. "I'm torn between Princess Diana and Marie Antoinette," she confessed. She smiled thoughtfully. "I don't just want a *costume*, you understand. I want to express my character, too."

Jessica smirked behind her sandwich. "How

about a butterfly, then?" she teased. "You do a lot of flitting around."

Lila gave her best friend a scornful look. Lila was used to being teased because she had a reputation as a flirt. Up until recently, being without a steady boyfriend had never bothered her. In fact, she enjoyed it. Lila enjoyed being popular. One of the benefits of being pretty *and* the daughter of one of the richest men in Sweet Valley was that you could pick and choose your dates. Lila, Jessica, and Amy used to be like the three musketeers of the Sweet Valley dating scene, flirting with every cute boy they met and going out with most of them. But now Amy had Barry, and Jessica had Sam. In fact, ever since Jessica and Sam Woodruff became such an item, Lila had begun to notice exactly how many couples there were in the world. Zillions. You couldn't turn around without tripping over one, gazing soulfully into each other's eyes. She seemed to be surrounded by people who were always doing things together, who talked about "we" all the time. Jessica especially had always been available for the spur-of-the-moment movie or shopping trip, but lately even she was always busy with Sam. And couples, Lila was also realizing, were taken more seriously than girls who played the field. Even incredibly attractive and wealthy girls like herself.

"I don't really think that's very funny, Jessica," Lila snapped, unhappy that her own friends didn't take her any more seriously than anyone else did. "You never can tell, you know. I might just surprise you yet."

The other three girls exchanged a look.

"Oh, really?" asked Amy. "I wonder who we're talking about now."

"Let me think," said Jessica. She closed her eyes and put her hand to her forehead, pretending to concentrate. "Wait a minute—I'm getting an image. I see a boy. He's tall and thin. He has dark, wavy hair and green eyes . . ."

Rosa put her face in her hands. "Yes," she breathed. "Yes, I think I see him, too. He's sitting at a typewriter . . ."

"Oh, don't tell me!" Maria gasped.

"Yes!" cried Jessica excitedly. "Yes! I think it must be—"

"It's not John Pfeifer, is it?" Maria, Rosa, and Amy shouted together.

"Why . . . you're right! It *is* John Pfeifer, boy sports editor!" Jessica's eyes opened wide. She grinned. "How did you ever guess?"

Lila speared some salad with her fork. "You four are *so* funny," she drawled. "Remind me to laugh, will you?" But though she acted annoyed, secretly Lila was pleased that they had noticed all the attention John had been paying her lately. Over the past few weeks she and John, who was the sports editor of the school newspaper, *The Oracle*, had been spending quite a bit of time together. They hadn't actually gone out on a date yet, but he always seemed to be around. If she wasn't bumping into him in the hallway or at her locker, she would find herself walking across the parking lot with him, or running into him when she was coming out of class. John had recently broken up with Jennifer Mitchell, whom he had been dating for a long time, so Lila had reason to think he might be seriously interested in her.

"Well, I think John's very nice," put in Rosa quickly. "Very polite and well-mannered."

Amy smirked. "You make him sound like a butler," she teased.

Jessica tossed her sun-blond hair over her shoulder and stared straight at Lila. "Well, I, personally, can't believe you'd even consider going out with John," she said. "He's not your type at all." An impish grin turned up the corners of her mouth. "Let's face it, Lila. If boys were automobiles, you usually go out with Corvettes. John's more like a Volvo with an air bag."

"And exactly what do you mean by that?" asked Lila. It was true that John wasn't like most of the boys she had dated in the past. He wasn't rich, or spectacularly handsome, or a big man on campus. Girls weren't lining up to date him, that was for sure. But in a way it was his ordinariness that made him appealing. John was an all-around nice guy who was hardworking, talented, and liked and respected by just about everyone. Exactly the sort of guy who usually found Lila frivolous and spoiled.

Jessica gave her a mocking look. "He's so serious, Lila. All he ever does is work. What could you two possibly have in common?" Jessica continued. "If you ask me, John Pfeifer is the sort of boy *Elizabeth* would fall for—that is, if Todd weren't in the picture."

Lila grimaced. Although Jessica and Elizabeth had the same California-blond beauty, the same blue-green eyes, the same perfect size-six figure, and the same dimple in their left cheek, they were identical only in looks. Jessica was the fun-loving twin whose schemes were always getting her in and out of trouble. She was irrepressible and funny, and dedicated to enjoying herself. Elizabeth, on the other hand, was serious and studious. She wanted to be a professional writer someday, and got more pleasure out of spending time with her best friend, Enid Rollins, and her boyfriend, Todd Wilkins, than she did in having a busy social life. Jessica was Lila's best friend; Lila had absolutely nothing in common with Jessica's sister. Nothing, that is, except for John Pfeifer.

"I'll have you know that I'm not just a pretty face," she said archly. "Just because I like to have a good time doesn't mean I'm not a serious person myself, you know."

"Oh, sure," said Jessica. "Very serious about shopping."

After school, Lila drove her lime-green Triumph into town to pick up some things for her big party. It was a warm, sunny afternoon, so she parked in the lot at the far end of town and walked down to the card and party shop. Even Lila herself would admit that she didn't normally have much more on her mind than what she was going to wear, or where she was going to go, and with whom she was going. This afternoon, however, was different. This afternoon Lila wasn't thinking only of party decorations and the menu for the buffet. This afternoon Lila had John Pfeifer on her mind.

She smiled as she thought about him. He had an intense manner that she wasn't used to, but that she was finding herself drawn to nonetheless. *I guess maybe opposites really do attract*, Lila thought as she strolled down the street. She liked John's attentiveness and the way he listened seriously to what she said. She liked his lopsided grin, and the way his eyes looked right into hers when they were talking. She liked the fact that he, unlike some people she could think of, people who considered themselves her close friends, didn't think she was superficial or flighty. He was kind and sympathetic, and he was always complimenting her and telling her how smart he thought she was. Lila caught her reflection in a store window. She was used to being told how pretty she was, but not how smart. Lila gave herself an approving smile. It wasn't that John made her feel special. Lila already *knew* she was special. It was that he made her feel that it wasn't just her beauty or her money that attracted him, it was the sort of person she was underneath.

Lila moved on, a tiny frown line appearing between her brown eyes as another, less happy, thought occurred to her. For, despite what she told the others, Lila did have some strong reservations about *The Oracle*'s sports editor. His seriousness and earnestness, as much as she was attracted to them, also made her a little nervous. She was used to boys who took things lightly, and who treated relationships as casually as she did. Sometimes, when she was with John, she wasn't really sure what to expect. He seldom talked about Jennifer Mitchell or their breakup, obviously shying away from the subject whenever Lila broached it. But when he did say something about Jennifer, the deepness of the hurt and anger he obviously felt about her made Lila uncomfortable. Just yesterday Lila suggested to John that he and Jennifer might be able to go back to being friends some day, and he had instantly become furious. "Not in this lifetime!" he shouted. When he saw the shocked look on her face he realized he had overreacted and recovered himself right away, but Lila still found the memory disturbing.

She came to a stop in front of the party-supply shop. *Should I get silver or purple paper plates?* she wondered as she stared at the bright and cheerful window display. She was just thinking that maybe she would get half silver and half purple when she realized that someone was smiling at her in the glass. She raised her eyes. There, reflected in the window of Party Paradise, was John

Pfeifer himself, standing behind her, so close it almost looked as though they were holding hands. Unasked and unexpected, a warm glow spread through her.

Lila turned around slowly. "Why, John," she said, managing to keep her manner slightly aloof and casual. "How long have you been standing here?"

"I saw you from across the street," he explained, "and I just had to come over. I've had some great news, and you're just the person I wanted to share it with."

There was something about the way he was looking at her that made her blush. An unaccustomed thrill of pleasure rushed through her. She moved so that she lightly brushed his arm with her hand. "Well, tell me," she said in her most coaxing voice. "Don't leave me in suspense."

"Not here," John said quickly. "Why don't we go for coffee? I was thinking we could try out that new café."

All thoughts of silver and purple plates went out of Lila's head. She gave him one of her best smiles. "You know, I've been wanting to try it. I hear the flavored coffee's very good."

"Only the best for you," John said.

Somehow, though neither of them moved, their fingers touched. "I know," she purred, her eyes on his.

They talked about school and the weather and the chances of the basketball team in the upcoming league tournament as they walked along. Once they were seated in the café, however, John couldn't contain his excitement any longer.

"You're not going to believe this," he boasted, his eyes shining with pride. "I didn't believe it myself." He shook his head. "I mean, I know I'm good," he went on, "but this is incredible!"

Lila couldn't get over the transformation. Usually John was so quiet and reserved. This was the first time she had ever heard him sound like a talking ego. "Why, John," she drawled, finding this new side of him undeniably attractive. "What is it? Don't tell me they're holding the next Olympics in Sweet Valley and you've been asked to cover it."

He shook his head. "Close." He grinned. He took a deep breath. "I've won a special internship with the sports department of the *L.A. Sun*! Isn't that great? They only give out a couple a year and you've got to be really excellent to even be in the running."

Lila's doubts about John began to drift away like clouds. An internship with the *L.A. Sun* was no small accomplishment. John might not be a football star or a TV personality, but a boy who won an honor like this was definitely going somewhere. Impulsively, she leaned over and gave him a hug. "John," she gushed. "I think that's just wonderful. I'm really proud of you."

This time it was John who blushed. "I knew you'd be pleased," he said. His gaze went from her face to the sugar bowl on the table between them. She could see that he was struggling to find the right words. "It's just that I . . . I really needed this, you know."

"Oh, I know," said Lila, unused to so much open emotion. "I know how much you want to be a professional sportswriter."

He raised his eyes to her again. "It's not just that," he said softly. "When Jennifer and I broke up . . . well, I cared for her so much that I think my self-esteem really took a beating."

"Jennifer? You shouldn't feel bad about Jennifer, John," Lila said gently. "There are plenty of other fish in the sea."


"Oh, come on, Sam!" Jessica sighed. "Stop being so stubborn. I think we'd make a perfect Romeo and Juliet." She held his arm. "Wouldn't you be willing to die for my love?"

Sam turned the car into Calico Drive. "Dying's one thing," he said. "Wearing tights is another."

Jessica gave him a punch. "Sam Woodruff. You told me there was *nothing* you wouldn't do for me."

"Except wear tights." He pulled to a stop in front of the Wakefields' split-level house. "That's the one thing I won't do, not even for you, my little spark plug."

"But, Sam . . ." She leaned her head on his shoulder.

"No, Jess, I mean it."

She put her arm around him. "Sam," she coaxed, "think of what a beautiful Juliet I'd make."

11

He turned so their faces were almost touching. "Then it'll have to be Juliet after Romeo's already dead, because I'm not running around in public in a pair of your pantyhose, and that's all there is to it."

She gave him the tiniest of kisses. "You're sure?"

He kissed her back. "I'm very sure."

She kissed him again, but this time the kiss wasn't quite so small. "Positive?"

His arms enfolded her. "Positive," Sam whispered, barely moving his lips from hers. "Absolutely certain."

Jessica could feel herself melting in his embrace. *Who cares about Romeo and Juliet?* she thought as their kisses became longer and more urgent. *If we'd lived first, they'd have been going to a masquerade as Sam and Jessica.*

The kissing went on and on. She never wanted to stop. She wanted to kiss Sam forever. Her mother could come to the door and call her, but Jessica wouldn't move. Her teachers could come by the car and shout at her to get to school, but she would keep right on kissing Sam. Elizabeth could come by and tap on the window, looking at her watch, but she and Sam would pretend they didn't hear her. "Elizabeth?" Jessica would whisper. "Elizabeth who?"

The longer they stayed in each other's arms, the more Jessica felt herself slipping away. She was no longer in the front seat of Sam's car on Calico Drive, she was floating in the sky of a sunny day. She and Sam, so close she could feel him breathing, as warm and strong as a kiss themselves.

Sam pulled back at the same moment as Jessica. Still holding on to each other, they sat for a few minutes, trying to regain their composure. Jessica's heart was racing.

Sam leaned against the headrest. "You know what I think we should go to Lila's party as?" he said once he had finally caught his breath.

Jessica stared out at the street. "What?"

He squeezed her hand. "A nuclear bomb."

Jessica didn't smile. This wasn't the first time something like this had happened. Lately, every time the two of them kissed it was harder and harder to stop. "This is serious, Sam," she told him once she had caught her own breath. "I'm really getting worried about this. What if I lose control?"

Sam put an arm around her shoulder. "What are you talking about, if *you* lose control? You're not the police force here, Jess. We're both involved. Nothing's going to happen if we don't want it to, and we don't. Just because we like kissing doesn't mean we're going to go too far. We've discussed that already."

Jessica leaned against him. "I know that, but I can't help feeling that it's up to me. I mean, I'm the girl. If I can't keep myself, you know, more in check, how can I expect you to?"

Sam moved his face in front of hers. "Jessica Wakefield," he said gently. "I may be a boy, but

I'm not some sort of wild beast, you know. It's not like you kiss me and I go brain dead right away. I'm a person, too. I have as much responsibility for what happens between us as you do." He kissed the top of her head. "I care about you, Jess. You know I would never hurt you."

She smiled back at him. "Does this mean you'll wear the tights?"

Jessica walked into the living room, relieved to see that her parents were out. She didn't really feel up to talking to them right now. Despite Sam's reassurances, she was still worried. No matter what he said, she couldn't shake the idea that it was up to her to be the one who never got carried away.

Lost in thought, Jessica climbed the stairs to her room. She could hear her twin sister Elizabeth talking on the phone in the adjoining room.

Jessica loved her sister dearly, but she also thought that Elizabeth was so levelheaded and reliable that she was boring. And Elizabeth was always trying to give her advice she didn't want to take. Now, however, it occurred to Jessica that Elizabeth might have some advice she would be willing to listen to. As soon as she heard her sister say good night to Todd and hang up the phone, she walked into her room.

"How do you two do it?" she demanded without any preamble. "That's all I want to know. How do you do it?"

Elizabeth looked up with a smile. "Do what?

Talk on the phone? It's easy. Todd dials my number, I pick up the receiver—"

Jessica took a stuffed toy from the dresser and threw it at her sister. "This is serious, Liz," she said. She flopped down on the foot of Elizabeth's bed. "How do you and Todd stay so close and not ... you know. The other night Sam and I were kissing so hard that we fell out of the car."

Elizabeth laughed.

"Fell out of the car?" she gasped. "How did you manage that?"

Jessica frowned. "I don't know. I guess I'd started to open the door and then I got distracted and ..." She sat up. "Elizabeth, will you please stop laughing? This isn't funny. Once I start kissing Sam I practically forget what planet I'm on."

Elizabeth gave her a shrewd look. "And you think Todd and I don't?" she asked. "You think Todd and I just shake hands and give each other a peck on the cheek?"

Jessica tried not to let her surprise show in her face. The idea of Elizabeth and Todd having as much fun kissing as she and Sam did was a new one to her. She always thought Todd and Elizabeth were about as exciting together as Mr. and Mrs. Wakefield. "You do?"

Elizabeth made a face. "Yes, we do. Only we know what we want and we've set our limits. We know when to stop."

"That's just it," said Jessica. "I'm not so sure Sam and I do. I mean, I think we do ... Sam thinks we do ... but sometimes *I'm* not so sure."

An impish smile lit up Elizabeth's face. "Maybe you and Sam are spending too much time alone," she teased. "Maybe you should get involved in more group activities."

Jessica rolled over on her stomach. "Oh, sure," she said. "Like dog sledding. That way we'd not only be with other people, we'd be too cold to do anything if we weren't."

# Two

Jessica's bedroom door opened and Elizabeth's head appeared. "What are you doing, Jess?" she asked. "Don't tell me you're not ready yet."

Jessica, hunched over her desk with a determined expression on her face, didn't look up. "Go away," she said. "Can't you see I'm busy?"

Elizabeth sighed. "Jessica," she said with exaggerated patience. "I have to get to school early today. I want to go to the *Oracle* office before classes start, and you're still in your pajamas."

The point of Jessica's pencil snapped. "Elizabeth, please!" She turned to face her twin. "I have *got* to get this math homework done before we go or I'll be in this class for the rest of my life."

Jessica hated it when her sister looked at her the way she was looking at her now. It was exactly the look her mother gave her when Jessica forgot to do some tiny little thing like fix supper or walk the dog. *It must be genetic*, she thought. *Thank goodness I didn't inherit it!*

"What are you talking about?" asked Elizabeth. "I thought Sam came over last night to help you with it. The two of you were in the kitchen for hours."

Jessica avoided meeting her sister's eyes. It was true that Sam had come over last night to help her with her math assignment. And it was true that they had spent hours in the kitchen. The trouble was that it was very hard to concentrate on quadratic equations when the cutest boy in California was leaning over your shoulder with his cheek next to yours.

Jessica pushed a golden strand of hair out of her eyes and sighed. "Well, we did start to do it," she explained. "We really did. But then Sam had to come around the table to show me something in the textbook, and then I sort of turned to ask him a question . . ." She shrugged helplessly. "And the next thing I knew, Mom and Dad were pulling into the driveway and it was so late that Sam had to go."

A smile tugged at the corners of Elizabeth's mouth. "I knew Sam was fast on a dirt bike," she teased, "but this is ridiculous."

"Tell me about it," said Jessica sourly. "This really isn't funny anymore, Liz. I'm just as bad as Sam is. Every time I'm near him I want to kiss him. I'm like a moth to a flame."

"It seems to me that the problem isn't that you *want* to kiss him," said Elizabeth, still trying not to smile. "The problem is that you *do.*"

Jessica scowled. How could her sister joke at a time like this? And everyone thought that Jessica was the frivolous twin! "We're going to have to have a guard."

"Oh, sure," grinned her sister. "Maybe Grandma could come out to be your chaperone. I'm sure she'd love going to dirt-bike meets and dances."

Jessica smiled at the image of their grandmother sitting in the back of Sam's car while she and Sam said good night. "Well, *something* drastic has to be done," said Jessica. "We can't go on like this."

Elizabeth's expression became serious. "Jessica," she said in her most reasonable voice, "promise me one thing. Promise me you won't go overboard like you usually do. This isn't the mega-crisis you think it is."

"Overboard?" Jessica repeated. "When have I ever gone overboard?"

"Jess, we don't have five hours for me to stand here and list all the times you've gone overboard. All I'm trying to say is that this is no big deal. Todd and I have gone through exactly the same thing. Every couple does."

Jessica bit her lip. It was absolutely impossible that Elizabeth and Todd, two of the dullest people in Southern California, could have gone through what she and Sam were going through.

Elizabeth was wonderful, but a girl who can't go to sleep at night unless she's written in her diary is not the sort of girl who is likely to be swept away by passion. And as for Todd—Todd was less exciting than a plate of cold potatoes. "No, you haven't," said Jessica shortly. "Nobody has."

"Jessica, listen to me. You don't have to go to extremes here. You just have to be a little more disciplined. At least get your homework done before you start to kiss."

"I'm not going to go to extremes, Liz," Jessica snapped. "I'm just going to get out of the way of temptation for a while." She had thought about it the previous night after Sam left, and again that morning. From that moment on, she and Sam would go everywhere in groups. When they kissed good night, they would kiss good night at the front door, under the porch light. When they held hands, they would hold hands in public places only. "As long as we're never alone, we'll be fine."

"It's going to be pretty crowded in Sam's car with half of Sweet Valley High in the backseat," Elizabeth said as she turned to go.

Elizabeth stopped outside the *Oracle* office. Inside, she could hear someone talking. "Well, you know what girls are like," a boy's voice was saying bitterly. "They never know what they want. They tell you one thing, and then they get mad at you when that's what you do." Could that be John Pfeifer? Elizabeth, her hand on the knob, hesitated. She had never heard that tone in John's voice before. There was a mumbled response from someone else, and then the door opened suddenly and one of the basketball players came out, calling goodbye and nodding to her as he passed.

Feeling a little puzzled by the belligerence she had heard through the door, Elizabeth walked into the office. John Pfeifer was sitting at his desk, a paper in front of him. He looked up with his usual warm smile. "Hi, Elizabeth!"

*Maybe I didn't hear him right*, Elizabeth thought. *Maybe he was reading from that copy of the daily paper.* She smiled back. "John!" she cried. "I was hoping I'd run into you. I wanted to congratulate you on getting the internship."

"Thanks, Liz," said John with a shy but happy grin. "I knew you'd be happy for me."

She threw her books down. "Well, if you knew I'd be happy, John Pfeifer, why didn't you tell me yourself?" she asked with a laugh. "I can't believe that I had to hear the news from Jessica, who heard it from Lila."

Elizabeth had been half kidding, but much to her surprise John started to blush. Elizabeth had to hide her surprise. Jessica had said she thought there might be something going on between Lila and John, and now it looked like she may have been right.

"I really haven't seen you since I heard," he mumbled. "I mean, I've been busy, and you've been busy, and . . ."

21

Elizabeth smiled. "But you have seen Lila."

John pretended not to know what she was getting at. "Oh, yeah," he said quickly. "I saw Lila. I ran into her in town the afternoon I found out," He shrugged. "You know, I was so excited I just had to tell somebody."

"Oh, yeah," said Elizabeth, sitting down across from him. "I know." She got out her papers and started looking them over. "You and Lila seem to be getting pretty friendly lately," she went on, trying to sound casual.

John picked up the newspaper and held it in front of his face. "Well, you know," he said evasively, "we've had a few classes together and everything. She's a nice girl. She's not as stuck-up as some people think she is."

Elizabeth and John had been friends for too long for her to let him get away with this. She reached over and pulled the newspaper down. "John Pfeifer," she said with an impish smile, "don't think you can fool me. I've seen the two of you walking in the hallway together and talking at her locker. I'm not an ace reporter for nothing, you know."

John shifted nervously in his chair. "Oh, we're not . . . I mean, I like her and everything, but . . ."

Elizabeth couldn't hide the fact that she was pleased for him. Although he wouldn't discuss it at any length, she knew how down John had been since he and Jennifer split up. He was so serious and intense that his confidence had almost vanished completely. Lila Fowler had never been one of Elizabeth's favorite people, there was no denying that, but if she was the person John wanted, Elizabeth wasn't going to say anything against her. Maybe someone who was light and not into having a heavy relationship was just what John needed to help him get over Jennifer.

"But what?" she teased. "Lila is one of the prettiest and most popular girls in the school."

John shrugged. "But I'm not one of the handsomest boys." He smiled wryly. "Or one of the richest." He shrugged again. "I don't know. I almost asked her out yesterday, but then I got cold feet at the last minute. I mean, we're not even in the same league, are we? How can I expect a girl as popular and rich as Lila to want to date me? It's like a carpenter wanting to go out with a princess."

"Oh, come on, John," said Elizabeth. "Don't put yourself down." She put a friendly hand on his shoulder. "You may not be royalty, but you are one of the nicest boys around. And you're the only one who has an internship at the *L.A. Sun*."

John's expression became earnest. "Do you really think I have a chance, Liz? I mean, sometimes I think she really likes me, and then I think about the guys she usually goes out with ..." He made a face. "It's just that I don't think I could stand any more rejection right now. Not after ... well, you know, I just couldn't."

Elizabeth touched his hand. "Well, there's only one way to find out, isn't there?" she asked.

*   *   *

Lila pulled open the door of her locker a little more abruptly than she had planned. Two notebooks and her gym sneakers flew out. "What a day," she grumbled as she bent down to pick them up. "It hasn't even started yet and already I don't like it." Almost every day for the past few weeks she had bumped into John as she walked across the parking lot, but this morning there hadn't been any sign of him. After their coffee in town the other afternoon, she had expected him to ask her out. Instead, though he had come running up to her yesterday as if there were something he had to say to her, all they had talked about in the end was what his first piece for the *L.A. Sun* would be, and what color scheme she had finally decided on for her ball. Lila shoved the sneakers back into the locker, took out the books she needed, and slammed it shut. *Boys*, she thought. *No wonder I always played the field.* Grumbling to herself, she turned around and walked right into someone who was standing behind her.

"John!"

He was smiling but his eyes were serious. "I thought I'd walk you to your first class," he said quietly.

Lila was relieved that her laugh sounded more natural than it felt. "But we go in opposite directions," she reminded him.

"That's all right," he said, falling into step beside her. "I need the exercise."

*He's going to ask me out*, Lila told herself as they

slowly made their way down the corridor. She glanced over at him. The boys she usually dated were self-confident to the point of arrogance, but John at this moment looked nervous and shy. She edged a little closer to him, her arm just touching his. "Everyone's talking about your internship, you know," she told him. "You're practically a local hero."

His green eyes turned to her. "I don't know about local hero," he laughed, the shyness giving way to that pride she had seen in him the other day.

Lila shook her head. "No, it's true," she said. "Everyone thinks you're terrific. It's such an honor! Everyone's saying you're some kind of genius."

They came to a stop in front of her classroom. "But is that what you think?" he asked. "Or is it just what everybody else says?"

"It's what I think," Lila said, her voice a whisper.

The bell rang, and students started hurrying past them, into the room.

John took an audible breath. "Does that mean you'd be willing to go out with me tomorrow night?"

He spoke so fast that if she hadn't been waiting for it, she might not have understood him. "Tomorrow?" Lila had already turned down two dates just in case John did ask her out, but she frowned as though she were considering her busy schedule anyway. "Well, sure," she said at last. "Sure. I don't think I have anything else planned."

"Really? You will?" His smile was so openly happy that, impulsively, she gave him a quick kiss on the cheek.

"Of course I will." She smiled back. "But now I have to go or I'll be late."

Just as she shut the door behind her, Lila turned back to the hall. John was still gazing after her. She gave him a wink.

Lila glanced at herself in the glass of the cafeteria door before she went into lunch. She wanted to make sure that she looked her usual calm, controlled self. Which couldn't have been further from the truth. Lila didn't know how it had happened, but she was so excited about her date with John on Saturday that she hadn't been able to think of anything else all morning. Maybe it was that she liked him even more than she had thought. Maybe it was that he was so different from her usual boyfriends that it made him especially attractive. She just wasn't sure. The only thing she was sure of was the fact that everyone else would be very surprised. Everyone was making such a big deal about his internship and how talented and serious he was that she knew they would never imagine him being interested in her. *Lila Fowler and John Pfeifer?* they'd say. *But she's so superficial and he's so serious ... I guess there must be more to her than we always thought.*

26

Lila slowly crossed the lunchroom to the table where Jessica, Amy, and Caroline Pearce were already sitting. The fact was that she was so excited about her date with John that she had decided not to tell her friends about it right away. She was going to make them guess.

Lila slipped into the chair next to Jessica.

Caroline was talking about how much trouble she was having finding crinolines for her Scarlett O'Hara costume for Lila's ball. Amy wanted Jessica to taste her sandwich because she thought it smelled funny. Jessica was worried that she had a split end.

Lila tapped her fork against her plate restlessly. What was wrong with them? Hadn't they noticed that she had a secret she wasn't going to tell them? Wasn't even one of them interested in *her*?

At last Jessica stopped talking about her hair long enough to say, "So how about it, guys? Anyone want to go to the movies tomorrow night?" She looked around the table. "I thought it'd be nice if a bunch of us went to see that new comedy."

"We might be up for it," said Caroline. "I'll see what Jerry thinks."

"Sure," said Amy. "It sounds like fun. I'll talk to Barry."

Jessica turned to Lila. "Well?" she asked. "You want to come along?"

Lila pushed her food around on her plate in a bored way. She knew from years of experience that the surest way to get Jessica to ask you for information was to act as though you didn't intend to give her any. "I'm afraid I can't," she said, not meeting Jessica's eyes.

Jessica tilted her head in a way that meant she was thinking. "Why not?"

Lila speared one pea with her fork and slipped it into her mouth. "I'm busy."

Jessica rested her chin on her hand. "Busy doing what?" she asked.

Lila dabbed at her mouth with her napkin. "Well, if you must know," she said in a bored voice, "it just so happens that I have a date tomorrow night."

Amy, Caroline, and Jessica all looked at one another.

"Oh, really?" said Amy. "And with whom would that be?"

Lila shrugged. "Oh, someone . . ."

"It wouldn't be with someone whose initials are J. P., by any chance, would it?" guessed Amy.

Caroline looked at her. "J. P.?" she repeated. "You don't mean John Pfeifer, do you?"

Lila fought back a triumphant smile. Caroline was the biggest gossip in Sweet Valley High. She usually knew what was happening even before the people involved did. But this time, Lila was one step ahead of her.

Lila nibbled on a piece of bread. "Maybe it is and maybe it isn't," she said coolly.

Jessica gave her a poke. "Look at you!" she cried. "You're blushing. It is John! John Pfeifer's finally asked you out!"

Caroline leaned back in her chair. "I don't believe this! How long has this been going on? I had no idea you and John were interested in each other!" She shook her head, unable to hide her surprise. "He's really upwardly mobile. First he wins the internship, and now you!" She shook her head again. "Wait'll I tell everyone. John Pfeifer and Lila Fowler ... what a story!"

"Have you asked him to your costume ball yet?" asked Amy. "Or are you playing hard to get?"

Jessica grinned mischievously. "You could go as Superman and Lois Lane," she suggested.

"So is this going to be a real item?" asked Caroline. "Are you two serious? Or is this just another Lila Fowler one-date wonder?"

A picture of her and John, holding hands and smiling, suddenly came into Lila's head. They were walking along a moonlit beach. She could almost hear music playing behind them. She could hear herself saying to her friends, "I'm afraid I can't go shopping, John and I already have plans." She could hear herself saying, "I'll have to check with John. We might want to come." She fought back a smile. Maybe it *would* be nice to have a real boyfriend for a change.

"Don't be silly," said Lila airily. "Saturday night's our first date."

"I'll call you first thing Sunday morning," Jessica promised.

At the other side of the cafeteria, Elizabeth, Todd, Enid, Olivia Davidson, and Dana Larson were having lunch together. Like most of their friends, they were also talking about Lila Fowler's masquerade party.

"You'd think it would be simple," Elizabeth was saying, "but Todd and I just can't agree on what we want to go as." She gave him a look. "That is, Todd can't agree."

Todd shook his head good-naturedly. "I just don't understand why you want to go as Antony and Cleopatra, Liz. I think a horse would be a lot more fun."

"A horse!" Enid nearly choked on her juice.

Olivia grinned. "I was thinking of going as something a little unusual ..." She shrugged. "You know, a tube of paint, or maybe a cloud or something ... but a horse?"

Elizabeth winced. "You want to go to Lila Fowler's costume ball as a horse?" asked Elizabeth, her lovely blue-green eyes wide with astonishment. "Are you kidding?" She folded her arms. "And just which end of the horse am I supposed to be?"

"I don't see what's wrong with a horse," Todd protested. "I always wanted to be one when I was little."

"But you're not little now," Elizabeth reminded him.

Enid made a face at Elizabeth. "Maybe Todd and Hugh should get together," she suggested. "Hugh seems to want to go as a chicken for some reason."

"Fried or roasted?" teased Olivia.

Elizabeth kept her eyes on Todd, trying to figure out what was going on inside his handsome head. It never ceased to amaze her that no matter how well you knew someone, they could still surprise you, like by wanting to dress up as a horse.

Enid laughed. "I think it's a Rhode Island Red, actually. It has something to do with his grandmother's farm when he was a child."

"Well, that is *not* the case with Todd," Elizabeth said. "Todd's grandmother has always lived in the suburbs. It's hard to imagine her fitting a horse in the garage beside her compact car!"

Todd threw his balled-up napkin at Elizabeth.

"Thank goodness Hugh's grandmother didn't own a pickle factory," joked Olivia.

The entire table burst into giggles. Wiping the tears from her eyes, Elizabeth suddenly realized Dana was being very quiet. She seemed to be miles away. Elizabeth smiled. "What about you and Aaron?" she asked. Aaron Dallas was Dana's boyfriend. "Have you decided yet what you're going as?"

Dana began to carefully cut her spaghetti into tiny pieces. "I was thinking of Sean Penn and Madonna," she said sourly.

"But Sean Penn and Madonna aren't a couple anymore," said Todd. "They broke up years ago."

"Exactly," said Dana.

Elizabeth couldn't believe her ears. She was the

one who had gotten Dana and Aaron together in the first place. "Don't tell me you and Aaron are having trouble," she said with genuine concern.

Dana gave her a look. "Is the Pacific Ocean deep?"

Jessica took the mail out of the box on her way into the house on Friday afternoon. "There's a postcard from Steven," she called excitedly as she walked into the kitchen.

Elizabeth, searching through the refrigerator for a snack, looked over her shoulder. "What's he say? Is he coming home for a weekend soon?" Steven Wakefield, the twins' older brother, was at college and only occasionally made it home for a visit.

Jessica smiled wickedly. "He says he's too busy at the moment," she said. Her eyes sparkled. "He says he finally decided to join the ski team, and that Jana, the captain, has offered to give him some extra help."

Elizabeth grinned. Steven had been devastated when his girlfriend, Cara, had moved to London. The twins had wondered if he would ever get over her. "I guess maybe Steven's really recovering at last," Elizabeth said happily.

"So long as he doesn't break a leg, he'll be fine," Jessica joked. Jessica sat down at the table, sorting through the rest of the mail. "Hey, what's this?" she asked Elizabeth as she slipped into the chair across from her. She held up an airmail envelope. It was expensive cream-colored stationery, embossed with a gold crest. "Don't tell me this is another letter from Prince Arthur?"

A slight flush of pink colored her sister's face. "What's so surprising about that?" she asked innocently. "You know we've been corresponding for years."

Jessica looked skeptical. It was true that Elizabeth and Arthur Castillo, the Crown Prince of Santa Dora, had been writing to each other on and off since he had visited Sweet Valley four years ago, but it had been a lot more off than on—until lately. "It used to be one letter a year at Christmas," Jessica pointed out. "Not one a week." She smiled wickedly. "I should have thought you'd have had enough letter writing for a while," she teased.

"Please," said Elizabeth, meeting her sister's smile with a rueful one of her own. "Don't remind me about our letter-writing business. You and your crazy ideas!" She made a face. "It nearly ruined my relationship with Todd."

"And this couldn't?"

"Of course not," said Elizabeth confidently. "Todd knows Arthur and I are just friends."

"Even so," Jessica said, "I do think it's pretty amazing that Todd doesn't get just a tiny bit jealous when you receive letters from another boy."

Elizabeth set the juice on the table with a laugh. "Jealous? What does Todd have to get jealous about? He knows I love him."

Jessica brought down the glasses. "Sam knows I love him, too," she said. "But that doesn't mean he'd be really happy if I were pen pals with a prince."

"Well, maybe that's why you don't feel you can be left alone with Sam anymore," Elizabeth teased in return. "Maybe he's too emotional. Todd, on the other hand, is completely levelheaded."

Jessica picked up the envelope and stared at it thoughtfully. "Or maybe he just doesn't know that this is the second letter you've had in two weeks."

# Three

Elizabeth looked up at the clock on the wall of the kitchen. Two hours had passed since Todd had arrived to spend the Saturday working on their costumes for Lila's ball, and they still hadn't decided what they were going to be. She suggested Napoleon and Josephine, and he suggested going as a set of salt and pepper shakers. She thought George and Martha Washington might be a cute idea, but Todd thought a pair of dice sounded cuter. If they couldn't come to some agreement soon, they would wind up going to the party as themselves.

Elizabeth turned back to Todd with a sigh. "I don't understand why this is so difficult," she said. "Let's just pick something so we can get started on making it. It hardly matters what it is at this point."

"Don't look at me, Liz," said Todd, as reasonable as ever. "I'm doing the best I can. I've told you my ideas—"

"Todd," said Elizabeth, also sounding very reasonable, "I do not think that a set of salt and pepper shakers is the best you can do. This party is a big deal. I want to go as something really dazzling."

"Really dazzling?" Todd frowned in concentration for a minute, and then, as a smile slowly spread across his face, he snapped his fingers. "I've got it, Liz!" he announced. "This time I've really got it!"

Elizabeth leaned back in her chair. "I'm afraid to ask."

Todd smirked. "You are going to love this," he assured her. "You are really going to love this." He paused dramatically, rubbing his hands together. "Ready?"

Elizabeth nodded. "I'm as ready as I'll ever be."

"A cowboy and a dancehall girl!"

Elizabeth stared across the table at him. She and Todd had been together a long time. He knew her better than anyone, except Jessica. She loved him. But at moments like this she wondered if she would ever understand him. "A cowboy and a dancehall girl?" she repeated. "You want *me* to dress up as a dancehall girl?" She leaned toward him. "Todd, I'd rather be the back end of the horse."

The smile vanished from his face. He looked confused. "But, Liz—"

"Todd, I am not the dancehall-girl type. I

36

should've thought you'd know that. Now if you want to go with Jessica . . ."

Todd made a face. "I don't want to go with Jessica, Liz. But at this rate, I won't be going with anyone."

Elizabeth was about to say that if he weren't so stubborn about George and Martha Washington there wouldn't be any problem, when Jessica herself charged into the room.

"Mail call!" she cried. She waved a cream-colored airmail envelope over her head. "Another letter from your prince," she said to Elizabeth as she stopped at the table. She rolled her eyes and put the letter down. "That makes three."

Elizabeth looked down at the envelope, resisting a sudden urge to kick her twin. Why did Jessica always have to make such a big deal of everything?

Todd grinned. "What's this? The dog is writing you letters?"

"Not Prince Albert," corrected Jessica, referring to the Wakefield's golden labrador. "Prince *Arthur*."

Todd looked at Elizabeth. "Who?"

"You remember him, Todd. My friend Arthur Castillo. He's thinking of coming to Sweet Valley for another visit, so he's been writing a little more than usual lately."

"Three letters in how long?" asked Todd.

Jessica answered immediately. "Two weeks."

Todd frowned. "What's he writing, a book?"

Elizabeth glared at her sister. "Arthur and I have a special friendship, Todd, you know that."

37

Todd leaned back in his seat, folding his arms across his chest. "And just how special is it?"

A car horn sounded outside. "Oh, there's Sam," said Jessica, already halfway to the back door. "I'll see you two later."

Neither of them watched her leave.

"I don't believe this," said Elizabeth as the door banged shut. "You're jealous. How can you be jealous of someone I haven't seen in four years? Someone who lives thousands of miles away?"

"I just think it's a little strange that he's writing you so much, that's all," said Todd. "It's not normal."

Elizabeth sat up a little bit straighter. "What are you saying, Todd? That Arthur has some ulterior motive?"

He shifted uncomfortably in his chair. "You must know what guys are like, Liz. They don't do things for no reason. You can't convince me he's writing to you so much because he wants to use up his Christmas stationery."

Was it her imagination, or was Todd's tone just a little patronizing? "I think I can write to an old friend without making him think I'm interested in him," she said stiffly. "Unless you're suggesting that I've been leading Arthur on . . ."

Todd ran his hand through his hair. "Of course I'm not suggesting that."

"Then what are you suggesting, Todd? That I'm a child who has to be protected?" She eyed him coldly. "I can take care of myself, you know."

Todd sighed, smiling wryly. "I know you can,

Liz. I wasn't trying to say that I don't trust you or that you can't take care of yourself."

Elizabeth could tell Todd was sorry that he had overreacted, but she wasn't about to let him off so easily. "Or maybe you'd like to go to the party as a sultan and his harem girl," she snapped.

"This is ridiculous, Jess," said Sam, glancing at her in the rearview mirror. "I'm not your chauffeur, you know. Come back up front."

Jessica, sitting in the back, shook her head. She had started the drive to the mall in the passenger seat as usual. She had climbed into the car, shut the door, and leaned over to give Sam a hello kiss. The next thing she knew, the horn was blowing and her elbow was caught in the steering wheel. "No," she said sternly. "No temptation, that's our new motto."

Sam sighed. "Jessica, what could possibly happen while I'm driving?"

Jessica knew it was unlikely that they would get carried away while stopped at a red light. After all, it was impossible to get too close while wearing seat belts. But that wasn't the point. The point was in establishing a pattern of restraint, in setting the limits and sticking to them. "I just think we should take every opportunity to practice self-discipline," she explained again. "That way it'll become second nature."

Sam turned into the Valley Mall. "I don't know why you always have to take everything to extremes," he grumbled.

Jessica put a hand on his shoulder. "That's exactly what I'm trying not to do."

"You're lucky I'm crazy about you, you know that?" Sam said, with a smile.

"I know that," Jessica answered. And then, feeling a little reckless, she kissed the back of his head.

*Maybe if I had fewer clothes this would be easier*, Lila thought to herself as she tossed another dress onto the pile already on her bed. She had been going through her wardrobe all afternoon, trying to find the perfect outfit to wear on her date with John that night, but so far she had been unsuccessful. Everything was either too casual, or too formal. Too short, or too long. Too bright, or too dull.

Finally, Lila pulled a black Lycra dress from the closet and held it in front of herself. "Something sexy but not cheap," she told her reflection. "Something that will knock him off his feet, but still look very sophisticated." She cocked her head to the left and then to the right. This dress could be just the thing, she decided. If she added a string of pearls and her crushed-velvet jacket she would have just the effect she wanted: attractively feminine, but restrained.

Relieved that she had finally come to a decision, Lila hung the dress on the back of the door while she put on her makeup. She couldn't remember ever feeling this nervous about a date before in her life. She wanted everything to be perfect. Absolutely perfect. *Maybe I really am becoming an intense and solid person,* she thought as she pulled the black dress over her head. *Now maybe people will finally start taking me seriously.*

Lila put on the pearls and the jacket, and fluffed out her hair. She studied the effect in the mirror. Even at the risk of being immodest, she had to admit that she looked terrific. No, better than terrific. Lila gave herself one of her million-dollar smiles. She knew she looked gorgeous. She could not only stop traffic, she could stop a stampede.

Lila knew the moment she opened the door and saw John standing there with a single red rose in his hand that he thought she looked gorgeous, too. She knew because he told her so.

"I can't get over you," he said. "You are so beautiful. Really beautiful."

Lila gave him a playful shove. "I bet you say that to all the girls," she joked.

"No," said John solemnly. "No, I don't."

All through dinner he continued to tell her that she looked beautiful. Lila was used to being complimented—in fact, she expected it—but John's openness and obvious sincerity took her a little aback. *He isn't just saying it because he feels he has to,* she told herself as they sat gazing at each other over coffee. *He really means every word.*

John put down his cup with a gentle click. "I can't tell you how long it's been since I felt this happy," he said. "I never thought I'd enjoy being with somebody so much again." He looked at the tablecloth. "I never imagined anybody like you would enjoy being with me."

Lila smiled sympathetically. A few hints John had dropped over dinner had told her that his breakup with Jennifer had left him even more shattered and insecure than she had guessed. "Well, somebody like me does," she said softly. "I'm having a wonderful time. I really am."

"Maybe we could take a picnic to the beach tomorrow," he suggested. That shy look came back on his face. "Unless you have other plans, that is."

Lila shook her head. "No," she said, forgetting that she usually liked to play hard to get. "I don't have any other plans."

She smiled to herself. This was the fourth or fifth time John had said "we" in connection with something they might do in the future—tomorrow, or next week, or even two weeks from now—and she found that she liked it. She really did. She was beginning to understand the appeal of belonging to a couple. It gave you a sense of security, of being wanted.

"Great." John beamed.

Lila held her breath for a second. She knew they were going very fast for a first date, but she didn't seem to be able to stop herself. "But only if you'll say you'll be my escort for my costume ball next Saturday," she said. "Please."

John reached across the table and touched her

hand. "It's a date. Amphibious tanks couldn't keep me away."

Lila couldn't remember when she had had such a romantic evening. First the candlelit dinner at the Box Tree and then dancing afterward under the stars.

"Look," John whispered as the last dance ended. "The moon's smiling at us."

If it had been any other boy, or any other night, Lila would have thought that was the corniest line she had ever heard. But tonight it sounded just right. She moved a little closer to him. "Why don't we go for a drive?" she whispered.

"What a wonderful idea," John whispered back.

Lila knew when she suggested going for a drive that the place they would be driving to was Miller's Point. Where else would a couple who liked each other so much they couldn't stop smiling on a night that was bright with stars and bathed in moonlight go?

"Good," said John as he stopped the car at the end of the Point with the most romantic view. "We have the place to ourselves."

Lila unsnapped her seat belt and turned to him, amazed at how her heart was pounding.

"Beautiful," John said softly.

"I know," said Lila. "It's a wonderful view."

He undid his own seat belt and leaned forward, reaching to put his arm around her. "I didn't mean the view," he whispered. "I meant you."

To Lila, a kiss had always been a kiss. You kissed your father and your friends on the cheek. You kissed a boy on the mouth. But kissing John was different. Her lips touched his, then touched them again. They were light, fleeting kisses at first; but then they began to linger. *I don't understand this*, she thought as he pulled her closer. *I've never been kissed like this before.* She felt a tingle race through her as she kissed him back. Was this Lila Fowler, being swept away like this? She felt as though she were glowing; as though there were nothing in the world but the two of them, bright as any star.

John kissed her again, and she kissed him back. He ran his hands down her back and she stroked the side of his face. *This is wonderful*, she thought, *this is really wonderful.* Their kisses became stronger, more urgent. She couldn't tell where one ended and the next began.

Somewhere, way at the back of her mind, a little voice began to call to her. *Lila*, the little voice was saying, *Lila, this is going too fast. If you don't stop now you're going to be sorry.* As soon as she heard it, Lila knew that the little voice was right. She pulled back gently, catching her breath. "John," Lila said, softly but firmly. "John, I think we'd better be getting home now. I do have a curfew."

Moonlight shone through the window behind him. "Just one more kiss," he breathed, pulling her back. "I can't tell you how good being with you makes me feel."

"Me, too," whispered Lila, sinking back into his arms.

One more kiss became another, and another, and another. The little voice in Lila's head was joined by the sound of warning bells. She began to slow down, trying to make her kisses as delicate and brief as they had been when she started, but John didn't slow down with her. She pushed the flat of her hand against his chest. "John," she insisted. "John, I really think we'd better stop. I have—I want to go home."

She expected him to laugh. She expected him to give her a hug and pull away. She expected him to say he thought they had better stop too, while they still could.

But he didn't.

"I don't want to stop," he said thickly, holding her tighter. "I want to keep going."

Lila had never been with a boy as intense and serious as John before, but she had also never been with a boy who wouldn't listen to her—with a boy she couldn't trust. She pushed a little harder. "I mean it," she said, her voice loud in the quiet of the car. "I have to get home. Now!"

"What's the matter?" His voice was loud, too. Loud and more forceful than she had ever heard it, all the tenderness of a few minutes before completely gone. "Don't you like me?"

A little afraid of the new tone in his voice, Lila said gently. "Of course I like you." She hoped her nervousness wasn't showing. "I like you a lot. You know that. But I have to get home."

"You'll get home," he assured her, starting to give her darting little kisses again.

Reassured, she began to return them. *Just a few quick kisses and then we'll stop and he'll take me home*, she told herself. *Just a few quick kisses, that's all . . .*

Without any warning, he kissed her so hard that her head banged against the door frame of the car. He didn't stop to ask her if she was all right, he didn't even seem to notice.

It was then that Lila realized that he wasn't going to stop, that he was completely out of control. "John!" she gasped. "John, stop! I mean it! Stop this second!"

He pressed her against the door. "Don't fight it," he ordered. "Just relax."

She struggled against him. "No, John! No!"

She wasn't sure if he even heard her. "You know you like it," he was saying, his voice low and urgent. "You know you don't really want me to stop." She heard him unbuckle his belt.

"Yes, I do," she shouted, panic overtaking her. "I want you to stop right now!" She shoved him so hard he hit the dashboard.

In the cool light of the moon, she could see that he was smiling at her. A chill ran through her. "Now you're teasing me," he said. "You shouldn't do that, Lila. You shouldn't tease."

Lila had heard of boys acting like this, but she had thought that was only in books and movies.

She had never thought that any boy she knew would behave like this. That any boy she went to school with, and talked to, and saw every day—and liked—could scare her so much. "Stay away from me!" she ordered. "I mean it, John!" This time, when his face came close to hers she slapped it as hard as she could.

He laughed.

*This can't be happening*, Lila told herself, her hand still stinging. *It can't be happening. Not to me.*

"I always knew you had a wild streak in you," he said, grabbing her by the hair and pulling her forward. "You like it, don't you, Lila? You wanted this to happen." His face was so close to hers she could feel him breathing. "But now you're trying to tell me that you don't. I hate it when a girl says one thing and then changes her mind."

A new coldness came over Lila. She fought back the tears that were welling up in her eyes. If she was going to get out of this, she was going to have to think. To think and act. And then she noticed the car keys. They were dangling from the ignition, just a few inches from her hand. If she could grab them she could use them as a weapon.

"You started this," said John, pulling her just that little bit nearer, just that little bit harder. "You can't stop now."

Not breathing, Lila snatched the keys from behind him and jabbed him hard in the neck.

"What are you doing?" He was so surprised that he let her go.

She wasn't thinking, she wasn't even feeling. She pushed open the door and staggered to the ground. She felt his arm reaching out for her, but she started swinging her bag at him. "Get away from me!" she screamed, her voice so shrill she couldn't believe it was hers. "Get away from me. I'm warning you!"

She saw him freeze, suddenly frightened. "Calm down," he said, trying to sound as he always did. "Get in the car, Lila, and I'll drive you home."

For one second, she almost believed she should get in the car and let him drive her home. But then she remembered his hands on her hair and the hardness of his voice just a few minutes before. "Don't you come near me!" she yelled. "Don't you ever come near me again!" With every ounce of strength she had, she took his car keys and threw them over the Point.

"You little witch!" he screamed.

But Lila was running down the road as fast as she could, her eyes streaming with tears. She heard him leave the car and start looking through the shrubs for the keys. *You'll be all right,* she told herself as she headed toward the main road. *He didn't hurt you. You'll be all right.*

She glanced up at the moon. It wasn't smiling anymore.

# Four

The morning sunlight streamed through Lila's bedroom window. Slowly, as though coming out of a trance, Lila opened her eyes. For a minute she lay there, trying to remember why she felt that there was something different about today. Her eyes moved from the tasteful wallpaper and the expensive curtains at the windows to the built-in shelves filled with her books and trinkets. Everything looked exactly the same. And then she saw her black dress and her crushed-velvet jacket, thrown on the floor in a heap like garbage.

Lila closed her eyes again as the events of the night before came back in a rush. A cold, unpleasant feeling crept over her, making her shiver in the warmth of her room. The last thing she remembered clearly was stopping at a gas station on the main road and calling a cab to take her home. Before that, she remembered running from Miller's Point and crying so much that she thought she would never stop. She remembered John's hands grabbing her and hurting her . . . the harshness of his voice.

She opened her eyes again, trying to push the memories away. *It couldn't have happened like that*, she told herself. *It just couldn't have. Things like that don't happen to real people . . . to people like me.* She brushed a strand of hair out of her face, and as she did so she noticed a red bruise on her wrist. *That's from when John wouldn't let me go*, she thought. *That's from when I was trying to get away.* She touched her cheek and felt the scratch made by his watch when he was holding her by the hair. She couldn't keep the memories from flooding back. As though someone had turned on a movie projector in her mind, the evening began to replay itself. She saw John and her driving up to Miller's Point, laughing and talking. She watched them kiss. She saw the kisses get longer and deeper. She saw herself pull away. And then she saw John pull her back to him. She heard herself screaming, "No, John! No! I want to go home!" She felt John's hands on her, pulling her closer, harder, refusing to let her go.

With a moan, Lila buried her face in her pillow. How could she have gotten herself into a situation like that? How could she have let it happen? John's voice whispered in her ear. *You like it, Lila*, it was saying. *You wanted it to happen.*

The telephone started ringing. Lila put her hands over her ears. She knew that it had to be Jessica, calling her as she had promised, to see how the date had gone. Had it been any other morning, Lila would have rushed to talk to her best friend. But not that morning. That morning she didn't want to talk to anyone, not even Jessica. There was a part of her that wanted to tell Jessica. That wanted to hear Jessica say everything really was all right. But she couldn't, she just couldn't. Somewhere in the back of her mind was the thought that if she didn't tell anyone at all what had happened, then it wouldn't be real. It would be as though Saturday night had never been.

The phone stopped ringing suddenly. A few seconds later, there was a gentle tap on her bedroom door. "Lila?" called Eva, the Fowlers' housekeeper. "Lila? Are you awake? Jessica's on the phone."

Lila stared at the door, willing Eva to stay on the other side. Eva had been with them for so long, Lila knew that she only had to look at her and she would know something was wrong. And suddenly Lila understood why she couldn't talk to Jessica. Not just because she wasn't sure that she could speak without bursting into tears, but because Jessica would know something was wrong right away, too, and Lila couldn't face the thought of anyone finding out what had happened. Not yet. Not when she didn't understand what had happened herself. She could hear John's voice again, whispering in her ear, *You started this, Lila. You want it* ... What if people didn't believe her? What if they were right?

She took a deep breath. "Tell her I'm not up yet," she answered, surprised that her voice sounded almost normal. "Tell her I'll call her back."

As she heard Eva's footsteps walk away and her voice talking on the extension at the end of the hallway, Lila knew exactly what she had to do. Nothing. *Just act like nothing happened,* she told herself, pulling the covers up around her. *That's all you have to do. Just pretend that last night never happened.*

Lila spent the rest of Sunday morning trying to act as though there had been no Saturday night. She took the clothes she had worn and threw them into the garbage. She took a long hot shower, trying to wash away the unclean feeling that seemed to cling to her. She put on the radio *and* the television so she wouldn't be able to think. When, later in the afternoon, the telephone rang again, she picked it up on the second ring, just as she would have done on any other Sunday. *See,* she told herself. *You're better already.*

Jessica didn't bother to say hello. "Why didn't you call me back?" she asked. "I've been waiting all morning."

"I was just about to call you," Lila lied. "I had a few things to do."

Jessica laughed. "Like talk to John Pfeifer

first?" she teased. When Lila didn't answer, she went on, her voice full of excitement. "Well? Come on, Lila, don't keep me in suspense. What happened last night? Was it the most wonderful date in the history of the universe, or what?"

Pretending that nothing had happened last night, that she had been out on a normal date, was going to be harder than she had thought. The words "or what" came to Lila's lips. She forced them away.

"It was OK," she said coolly. She could tell from her silence that Jessica was expecting to hear more. "He's nice, but he isn't exactly royalty, you know," she explained.

Jessica laughed. Lila couldn't get over how normal Jessica sounded. It seemed so strange to Lila that everything in Jessica's world was exactly the same that day as it had been the day before, when everything in *her* life had been turned upside down.

"I knew you wouldn't think John was good enough for you," Jessica joked. "What happened? Didn't he know which fork to use for his salad?"

Suddenly Lila knew that she couldn't keep this up any longer. Just the mention of John's name brought back that unclean feeling. "What about you?" she asked, abruptly changing the subject. "Did you and Sam finally decide what you're wearing to my party?"

"It's a secret," said Jessica. "All I'll say is that it's a compromise between motorcycle cops and Romeo and Juliet."

The last thing Lila wanted to hear about right now was Romeo and Juliet. Dr. Jekyll and Mr. Hyde, maybe, but not Romeo and Juliet. And all at once she realized that pretending wasn't going to be enough. Even if she could pretend to everyone else, she couldn't pretend to herself. An unexpected tear trickled down her cheek. "I've got to go, Jess," she said quickly. "I think my father's just come back from his business trip. I'd better go."

Lila hung up the phone, but her hand lingered on the receiver for a few minutes. She was half tempted to pick it up and call Jessica back, but what would she say? How could she explain what had happened last night? She imagined saying, "Jessica, John Pfeifer tried to rape me last night." And she heard Jessica laugh and say, "Oh, stop kidding around, will you, Lila? What do you think I am, gullible? John Pfeifer's one of the most serious and nicest boys at Sweet Valley High, not some lowlife who just crawled out from under a bush. He might have bored you to death talking about basketball, but he would never attack you. He's not like that."

Lila lay back on her bed. Maybe she *had* led John on. Maybe the whole thing had been her fault. After all, she was the one everyone considered flighty and irresponsible. She was the flirt. What if what John had said was true, what if she had encouraged him? She had liked the kissing, she couldn't deny that. And she was the one who had suggested taking a drive. People would say she should have known what to expect. Nice girls don't ask boys to take them to Miller's Point. Nice girls don't enjoy kissing as much as boys do. Nice girls don't kiss back.

Lila gave herself a shake. She couldn't let herself sink into this way of thinking. She remembered when Elizabeth wrote that article for *The Oracle* on the sexual harassment of students by teachers. Elizabeth had gone around asking all the girls if they knew what they would do if a teacher came on to them, and Lila could still remember her own answer. "Yeah," she had said. "A good swift kick should do the trick." She had to get that attitude back.

*You're not the first girl this has ever happened to,* she told herself. *It happens all the time. Look at the papers, every day there's a story like this. Look at all the shows you've seen on television.*

Lila sat up, and once again she reached for the phone. Deep in her heart, she knew exactly what she should do. She should tell someone. Amy was always talking about the counseling program she worked for, Project Youth. Project Youth was a community group that helped teenagers with all sorts of problems, from family trouble to the sort of thing that had happened to her. Amy had been a volunteer on the hot line for some time, and Lila knew that if she called them they would refer her to someone who could help her deal with what had happened to her. Her fingers touched the receiver. She could call them. They wouldn't need to know her name or the name of the boy. She could talk it through with someone. Someone who would reassure her it wasn't her fault. Someone who would advise her on what to do next.

Lila lifted the receiver and dropped it again as though it were hot. What if they didn't tell her it wasn't her fault? What if they said she should never have gone up to Miller's Point in the first place? What if they asked her what she had been wearing? "You were wearing a short black dress?" they would say. "Made of Lycra? Well, what did you expect?" What if the volunteer who answered recognized her voice? "Isn't that Lila Fowler?" the volunteer would say. "The biggest flirt in Sweet Valley High?"

Lila buried her face in her pillow and burst into tears.


"Isn't this great?" asked Jessica, striding briskly through the park with Sam and Prince Albert later that Sunday afternoon. She gave Sam a meaningful look. "Exercise is supposed to be very good for you when you have a lot of . . . you know, energy."

Sam picked up a stick and threw it for the golden labrador, who bounded after it with a happy bark. "I'm surprised you haven't suggested we take up bungee jumping then," said Sam. "That would not only keep us out of clinches, we'd probably be so bruised at the end of the day that we wouldn't even be able to shake hands good night."

Jessica gave him a playful shove. The fact that

Sam was so willing to go along with her new hands-off policy, even though he complained about it all the time, made her like him even more. She knew that if he didn't really care about her he wouldn't be loping ahead of her right now, looking for another stick to throw to the dog.

"You know we can *walk* together," she said when she finally caught up with him. "There's no rule against that."

Sam wiggled his eyebrows. "You mean you're not afraid I might try to kiss you right here in front of these hundreds of people with their dogs and their Frisbees?"

Jessica linked her arm through his. "I'll take my chances," she said with a laugh.

"Good." He gave her a wink. "So let's not talk about how much I would like to kiss you right here in the middle of the park. Let's talk about something neutral. How was Lila's big date with Mr. I'm-a-Serious-Sports-Reporter?"

A thoughtful look came into Jessica's eyes. "You know, I'm not really sure," she said at last. "Now that I think about it, she didn't say much at all. She sort of pooh-poohed it. You know what Lila's like. She made it sound like she was bored after the first five minutes. But, I don't know . . ."

Sam kicked a stone ahead of them. "Since I *do* know what Lila's like, I'd say that she probably *was* bored after the first five minutes." He grinned. "It's not easy being a princess surrounded by common folk, you know."

"Oh, stop," said Jessica. "She's not really that bad. And anyway, she was really looking forward to this date, I could tell. I can't believe it just fizzled out the way she said it did."

Sam looked over at her. "Jessica," he said with exaggerated patience, "if Lila says it was a dull date, then why can't you believe it was a dull date and leave it at that?"

"Because I'm her best friend, that's why." Jessica shook her head. "I called her first thing this morning, just like I said I would, and Eva told me she was still in bed."

"So?"

She gave him an exasperated look. "So Lila doesn't get up later on a Sunday than *I* do, Sam. And anyway, I could tell from Eva's voice that Lila was awake."

Sam groaned. "Jess, I'm begging you. Don't start using that imagination of yours."

Jessica's blue-green eyes were wide with innocence. "What do you mean, don't start using my imagination? This isn't imagination, Sam, this is knowledge. There's no one I know better than Lila, except Liz. I think I can tell when something is wrong, and I definitely think something's wrong."

Sam laughed. "Because she didn't get up till after noon?"

Jessica made a face. "No, because she didn't call me back. Even if it was a boring date, she would have called me back to give me all the dirt. It's not like Lila to be so reserved."

"There seems to be a lot of that going around right now," Sam teased.

Jessica ignored him. "I just have this feeling," she said. "I don't know why." She bit her lip. "But I'm sure something's not right."

Sam reached for her hand and gave it a squeeze. "It's always trouble when you have a feeling."

She slipped her hand from his and gave him Prince Albert's leash to hold instead. She smiled. "I know."

Enid pulled the wrapper off her straw. "I'm telling you, Liz," she said with a laugh, "I've never known anyone as stubborn as Hugh. No matter what I suggest for a costume, he keeps going back to that dumb chicken idea."

Elizabeth and Enid, tired of arguing with their boyfriends about what they should wear to Lila's party, had finally escaped together to the Dairi Burger for a little peace and quiet.

Elizabeth took a sip of her soda. "You think Hugh's stubborn?" She laughed. "You should hear Todd! Usually he's so agreeable and into compromise, but just mention George Washington to him and he digs his heels in the ground and won't budge."

Enid made a face. "I was so excited when I first heard about this party. I thought it would be a lot of fun. But now it's becoming a headache. If I can't get Hugh to change his mind pretty soon, I'll end up going as Colonel Sanders."

"Boys!" Elizabeth sighed. "Sometimes I really don't understand them. Not only won't Todd back down on our costumes, he's started giving me a hard time just because Arthur Castillo's been writing to me more than usual."

Enid raised one eyebrow. "Really?" she asked. "That doesn't sound like Todd. He isn't the jealous type."

Elizabeth shrugged. "I know. He's not the jealous type and there's nothing to be jealous of. I mean, Arthur Castillo lives thousands of miles away, I haven't seen him in four years, and we were never more than friends. Now, all of a sudden, Todd's suspicious because I've had a couple of letters."

Enid laughed. "You mean he thinks the prince is putting the moves on you via air mail?"

"Todd says no one writes a girl three letters in two weeks just because he likes to correspond."

"Why not?" asked Enid. "Didn't you say that Arthur might be coming for a visit? He's probably a little nervous and just wants to be in touch."

Elizabeth was glad she and Enid had decided to come out on their own. It was a relief to talk to someone who made so much sense. "Well, that's what I said, of course. But Todd seemed to think I was being naive."

Enid took a sip of her drink. "Do you think boys have brains like we do, or do you think there's something else up there under their skulls? Like a broken computer or something?"

"I have no idea." Elizabeth laughed. "It could be a video game for all I know."

"It is strange, though, isn't it?" asked Enid. "I mean, sometimes I'm surprised we even speak the same language."

"I'm not always sure that we do," Elizabeth said.

# Five

*If only this were last Friday,* Lila thought when she woke up on Monday morning. If it were last Friday, she would do everything differently. When John asked her out she would say that she was already busy. She would say that she was going to be busy for the rest of her life.

Lila turned to the alarm clock on the table beside her bed. The awful truth was that it wasn't Friday, it was Monday, and there was no going back. But that, of course, wasn't the most awful part of the truth. The most awful part was that she had to go to school today. And at school she would not only have to face Jessica and her other friends, all of them wanting to know what happened on her "big" date—she would have to face John as well.

At the thought of John, Lila moaned. She could see him clearly, standing in the corridor, leaning against the wall the way he did, talking to his friends. He would look at her when she passed him and he would grin. It would be a sly, knowing grin. He would look her right in the eyes, and he wouldn't say anything. He would just keep smiling, but his eyes would be saying, *You started it, Lila. You asked for it.*

"I'm not going to school, that's all," Lila announced to her empty room. "No one can make me." She would tell Eva she wasn't feeling well. She would say her head ached and her stomach hurt. She would claim that she was coming down with something. Something contagious that would keep her home.

*Keep you home for how long?* asked a voice in her head. *Today? Tomorrow? The rest of the week?* Lila closed her eyes. She might as well face it. Unless she came down with the bubonic plague, she was going to have to go back to school eventually. Staying away wasn't going to make it any easier. Staying away would make it worse. Perhaps if she went to school this morning, just like always, and walked down the hallway past John Pfeifer, just like always, and had lunch with her friends, just like always, then maybe by the end of the day it would really be as if nothing had happened.

"Lila!" Eva's voice called to her on the intercom system that her father had set up throughout the twenty-room mansion. "Lila! Your breakfast is on the table. You'd better get down here now!"

Lila hesitated for half a second. And then she threw back the blankets and slid out of bed. "Just act normal," she told herself as she went into her bathroom to wash. "Just act normal and you'll be all right."

For a change, Jessica was the first twin down to breakfast on Monday morning. She could feel her mother's eyes following her as she entered the kitchen and crossed to the refrigerator to get out the milk.

"You're up bright and early," said Mrs. Wakefield. "Didn't you sleep well last night?"

Jessica glanced over her shoulder. Her mother was watching her with what Jessica thought of as her Concerned Parent smile on her face. "Yeah, Mom. I slept fine."

"I just thought you'd be exhausted after all the help you and Sam gave me and your father yesterday when you got back from your walk in the park," Mrs. Wakefield explained.

Jessica took out the milk and went to sit down at the table. In order to avoid any possibility of their winding up in a clinch the previous afternoon, she and Sam had volunteered to help her parents clean out the garage. This meant that they lugged things out to the garbage with Mrs. Wakefield and made sure that Mr. Wakefield didn't sneak it all back in again. Jessica filled her bowl with cereal. "We were glad to do it."

Mrs. Wakefield picked up her coffee cup. "Your father and I were a little surprised, though," she said slowly. "Usually you and Sam can't wait to get away from us. You two practically carry a sign that says 'three's company.' "

Jessica concentrated on covering her cereal with milk. All the while they had been sorting through the old patio furniture and boxes of junk stored in the garage, Mrs. Wakefield had kept saying, "Any time you two want to go off by yourselves, you know you can." Jessica hadn't been able to believe her ears. Her own mother, encouraging her to be alone with Sam! You'd think there was some sort of conspiracy going on. What had happened to the good old days, when fathers locked their daughters in towers? Finally realizing that her mother was waiting for her to say something, Jessica said, "I really like this new cereal with the fruit in it. It's delicious."

"You know," said Mrs. Wakefield, "your father and I have always liked the way you and Sam are so relaxed and affectionate together." She sipped her coffee thoughtfully. "Your father thought that you seemed a little formal with each other yesterday."

Jessica hid her smile behind her spoon. The only thing her father had noticed yesterday was that his favorite five-year-old magazines were being thrown out. The person who had been noticing that she and Sam jumped apart every time they accidentally brushed against one another was her mother. "It's hard to be affectionate when you're dragging broken wicker chairs out to the garbage," she joked.

Mrs. Wakefield didn't laugh. "Nothing's ... um ... nothing's happened between you and Sam, has it, Jessica?" she asked.

*No, and nothing's going to,* Jessica thought. She looked at her mother, her eyes wide with innocent surprise. "Of course not," she said. "I don't know what you're talking about, Mom. Maybe all that dust affected your brain."

"Um," said Mrs. Wakefield, her expression thoughtful. "Maybe."

Lila couldn't remember a time when she didn't know that she was special. And knowing that you're special gives you certain advantages over other people. You never feel insecure. You never feel nervous. You never feel unsure of yourself. Normal for Lila Fowler was being as confident as a queen visiting the neighboring peasants. But as she approached the entrance to Sweet Valley High on that Monday morning, Lila began to realize that she might never feel normal again. For the first time in sixteen years she felt nervous, insecure, and unsure. She didn't know what to expect—not from anyone, least of all herself.

A few girls Lila knew greeted her as she walked into the building. Lila forced herself to smile and say hello back, just as she would have on any other day, but all the time her eyes were darting left and right, waiting to see John Pfeifer.

It was like watching a horror movie and waiting for the hand to come out of the darkness.

And then, all at once, there he was. He was walking with Aaron Dallas. Aaron was talking animatedly, but it seemed to Lila that John was moving toward her with a slow, deliberate step, looking straight at her. Lila froze. She had gone over this moment in her mind a hundred times since yesterday morning. Would he act as though nothing had happened? Or would he ignore her completely? It had even occurred to her that he might be waiting at her locker, full of excuses and apologies. "It was all a mistake," he would say. "I'm really sorry. I don't know what came over me. Can you ever forgive me?"

She had imagined what she thought was every possibility, but still she was unprepared for actually coming face to face with John. It wasn't that she was caught off guard, it was that there was nothing she could have done to protect herself from the contemptuous look in those green eyes. She felt as though she were a bug who had crawled across his path, and that if she didn't step out of the way he would squash her. But she couldn't get out of the way. All of a sudden her body was acting as if it had been bolted to the ground.

Aaron, noticing her standing there, nodded hello. "Hi, Lila." He smiled.

But John, his eyes not flinching, said nothing.

She couldn't return Aaron's smile.

And then, just as they passed her, John laughed. It was a harsh sound, completely without humor. A few heads turned.

Lila felt her face go red with shame. All of a sudden she was sure that everyone knew what had happened; that they could tell just by looking at her. That they could hear the voice she heard whispering in her ear. *You started it, Lila. You asked for it. You're a tease* ... She started walking again, as fast as she could.

"There she is!" shrieked Amy as Lila, walking so quickly she was almost running, came down the hall. Amy, Jessica, and Caroline were all standing in front of her locker, smiling as always.

Lila caught her breath. Though she was trying not to meet their eyes, she could see that Amy and Caroline were bubbling with excitement, but that Jessica was watching her closely, as though she had already guessed that something was wrong.

"Well, come on," Caroline was saying. "Tell us all about your date! We can't wait to hear everything that happened."

Jessica grinned. "She means she can't wait to tell everyone else."

"We can't get a word out of Jess," Amy complained. "She says we have to ask you."

"I told them you seemed to think it was about as exciting as buying flour," said Jessica.

Lila didn't look at them as she walked straight to her locker and began to fiddle with the lock.

"There's nothing much to tell," she said in a flat, lifeless voice, the only way she could hope to control the emotion she felt welling up in her. "Jess is right. It wasn't so great."

"Oh, no you don't," said Caroline. "We want details. We want to know every single thing that went on. And we won't let you go till we do."

Lila was glad her back was to them, because she could feel the color drain from her face at the thought of the details of Saturday night. Her hand shook as she opened the locker door, but she managed to make her voice steady. "I told you," she said, with something like her old coolness. "There's nothing to tell." She reached inside for the books she would need for her morning classes.

Amy laughed. "Don't think you can fool us, Lila Fowler," she said, leaning against the locker next to Lila's. "I saw John on my way in and he cut me dead. What'd you do to him? Hit him when he wanted to kiss you good night?"

The books in Lila's hand fell to the floor.

Jessica bent down to help her pick them up. "Are you all right?" she asked, real concern in her voice.

Lila kept her eyes on the ground. "Of course I'm all right," she snapped. "I just don't know why you guys can't leave me alone, that's all."

She could feel Jessica staring at her.

"We didn't mean anything," said Jessica softly. "Don't tell me it was John who didn't want to kiss *you* good night," teased Amy. "Is that what it was, Lila? Have you finally met the one boy who can resist your charms?"

Lila shot to her feet. "I've got to go," she said to no one in particular. "I've got a—a meeting." She turned on her heel and hurried down the hall without once looking back.

The three girls stared after Lila's rapidly retreating back. Caroline was the first to speak. "Well, what do you make of that?" she asked.

Amy shrugged. "Oh, you know Lila," she said lightly. "She can be really moody. It's part of being a princess."

"She seemed more than just moody to me," Jessica said slowly. The vague suspicions she had had before seemed even more real now. The girl who had just run away from them was not the cool, confident Lila Fowler who was her best friend. She didn't even look the same. Lila was always a careful dresser, concerned about how she looked. Jessica noticed not only was Lila wearing very little makeup, but she had on a dress that Mrs. Wakefield wouldn't even wear to the supermarket.

Caroline nodded. "Did you see the outfit Lila had on?" she asked, echoing Jessica's thoughts. "It's at least a year old. I think Jess is right. It's more than just a bad mood."

Jessica frowned as the three of them started toward their homerooms. If it wasn't just a bad mood, what was it? she wondered.

\* \* \*

Eva was coming through the hallway with an armload of clean laundry when Lila let herself into the Fowler mansion on Monday afternoon.

Lila smiled, but Eva was watching her closely. "You're not coming down with something, are you, Lila? You seemed very distracted this morning." She stopped in front of her. "And now you look a little pale."

"No," said Lila, hugging her books to her chest and hurrying past Eva up the stairs. "No, I'm fine."

"Because if you are I could make you some chicken soup for supper," Eva called after her. "There's nothing like homemade chicken soup when you're not feeling well."

In answer, Lila slammed her bedroom door shut behind her.

Once in the safety of her own room, Lila threw herself on the bed with a sob. Never in her life had she been so glad to get home. If she had had to spend one more minute at school she didn't know what she would have done. She pressed her face into her pillow, trying to make the world go away. All the chicken soup in the universe wasn't going to make her feel any better. She could drink chicken soup for the next fifty years and she was still going to feel as lost and disgusted with herself as she did at that moment.

How could she ever have thought, even for one second, that John was going to apologize to her? That he would say he was sorry, it had all been some sort of horrible misunderstanding, and everything would be all right again? How could she ever have thought that she could act as though nothing had happened and it would be as though nothing had? Even though she had tried her best to avoid him, she must have run into John at least half a dozen times throughout the day. And every time he had looked right through her.

Lila got up and went to stand in front of her full-length mirror. Looking back at her was the same pretty young girl with the long brown hair and thickly lashed brown eyes, but something had changed. Lila had never looked at her reflection without a smile of approval, but now she felt only shame. The truth was that she was beginning to feel as if she were made of dirt. "What if John starts talking about you?" she asked her reflection. "What then?" She gave herself a bitter smile. "I'll tell you what," she went on. "He'll tell everybody that you're easy, that's what. He'll say it was all your fault."

Lila recalled what had happened recently to Elizabeth with Kris Lynch. To get back at Elizabeth for not wanting to go out with him, Kris had spread rumors that they had gone to Miller's Point and that he had had to fight Elizabeth off. Everyone had believed him. If people could believe something like that about Elizabeth, a girl whose idea of a wild time was washing the car, then what chance would Lila have of ever convincing anyone that she was the innocent victim in all this? She gave herself another sour smile. She couldn't even convince *herself* at this point.

The ringing of the princess phone on her bedside table brought her attention back to the moment. Not wanting to arouse any more of Eva's suspicions about her health by not answering it, Lila went over and picked up the receiver.

"Lila Fowler," said Jessica in her no-nonsense voice, "I want to know what's going on."

Lila hadn't expected Jessica to take such a direct approach. She had expected her to beat around the bush a little, be sneaky, as she usually was. "What happened to 'hello'?" Lila snapped back, stalling for time.

"Never mind hello," Jessica replied. "You've been avoiding talking to me and everybody else all day long, and I want to know why. I want to know why you're so jittery. I want to know why you're acting so weird."

"Weird?" Lila repeated. "I don't know what you're talking about, Jess. I'm not acting weird."

Jessica sighed with exaggerated patience. "Lila, I'm your best friend. I'm begging you. If something's wrong . . . if something's happened—"

Tears welled up in Lila's eyes. If she didn't get off the phone in the next nanosecond, she was going to be out of control. "The bath!" Lila screamed. "I left the water running. I'll call you back, Jess. I can't talk now."

She slammed down the phone, and started to cry.

Despite her problems with being alone with Sam, Jessica was glad that they had arranged to work on their costumes together after school on Monday afternoon. Her brief phone conversation with Lila had left her both worried and confused, and it was a relief to have something to take her mind off it.

"Sam, could you give me a hand with this?" she asked. "I need you to pin me up." In the end, she and Sam had decided to go as Princess Leia and Han Solo from *Star Wars*.

Sam came up from behind and put his arms around her. "I'll pin you up any time you want," he said in her ear.

Jessica pulled away so quickly that he nearly fell.

"Talk about cold space," said Sam as she slapped the box of pins into his hands.

"I didn't tell you what happened with Lila today," she said, ignoring him. "She was so peculiar, Sam. I'm positive that something's happened. She isn't the same person anymore."

Sam jabbed a pin into the hem of her dress. "She isn't the only one," he said sourly.

But Jessica was determined to keep the conversation as far away from her and Sam as she could. "I just can't figure out what it could be, though," she continued. "It must have something to do with her date on Saturday, but unless John turns into a werewolf at the full moon, how bad could it have been?"

Sam put the box down and sat back on the floor. "I don't want to talk about Lila Fowler,

Jess," he said, looking up at her. "I want to talk about you and me. I really don't think I can take much more of this. You're making me feel like some kind of criminal. All I have to do is hold your hand, and you act like I'm attacking you."

Jessica felt a pang. It wasn't like Sam to be so stubborn. He usually respected her wishes, especially when it was something this serious. "It's just that I'm so afraid of losing control," said Jessica, sitting down on the floor across from him with an unhappy sigh.

He looked into her eyes. "Don't you trust me, Jess? I'm not some guy who wandered in off the street, you know. It's me, Sam, the nicest guy you've ever known."

Jessica couldn't help smiling. She took his hand in hers. "It's not you, Sam," she said softly. "It's *me* I don't trust."

"Well, *I* trust you. I'm sure you won't take unfair advantage of me."

Jessica laughed, but without her usual good spirits. When he squeezed her hand she didn't squeeze back.

Sam let go of her. "It's like there's some sort of glass wall between us," he complained. "If you won't let me act like your boyfriend, Jessica, then maybe we should just be friends for a while."

This was not what Jessica wanted to hear. Could Juliet have been friends with Romeo? Could Cleopatra have gone bowling with Marc Antony and not kissed him good night? On the other hand, though, what else could they do? "Maybe you're right," she said glumly. "Maybe we should just be friends."

"Great," said Sam. He held out his hand. "Let's shake on it, buddy."

Jessica pumped his hand heartily. "Maybe we picked the wrong costumes for the party," she said with a rueful smile. "Maybe we should have gone as R2-D2 and C-3PO."

Sam grinned. "No, we'll be fine," he assured her. "We'll tell them we're Princess Leia and Han Solo from the first movie. When they still didn't like each other."

Elizabeth happened to look across the cafeteria from where she, Todd, Enid, Maria Santelli, and Winston Egbert were having lunch together on Tuesday as John Pfeifer sat down at a table with several members of the basketball team.

"You know, it's the strangest thing," she said thoughtfully, "but when I asked John yesterday about his date with Lila he wouldn't even answer me. He just acted like I'd said something in Greek and started talking about his internship."

Enid, sitting across from her, looked surprised. "But I thought he was so excited about it. I thought it was a really big deal."

"That's what I thought, too," said Elizabeth. "But he was so weird about it that I didn't even try to press him."

Winston looked up from the mound of french fries he was wolfing down. "You know, that's funny," he commented. "I said something to him, too, and he practically bit my head off. Said Lila wasn't his type."

Todd shrugged. "Same thing happened to me. I asked him in gym this morning if they'd had a good time, and he told me he'd only gone out with her as a joke."

Elizabeth frowned at her sandwich. "Well, that's not the impression I had. When he first told me he wanted to ask Lila out, he sounded very serious. And Jessica said she thought they really liked each other."

"Not anymore," put in Todd. "Now he says she's just a flirt and even more shallow than everyone thinks."

"Oh, please . . ." Enid made a face. "She couldn't be *more* shallow."

Maria bit her lip. "It is strange, you know," she said slowly. "Lila won't talk about it, either. Usually she won't shut up about her dates, but I couldn't even get her to tell me where they went."

Elizabeth, Maria, and Enid all looked at each other, their eyes asking the same questions. Elizabeth knew that it was as obvious to her friends as it was to her that something was going on, but none of them could figure out what it was.

"I guess that's the way it goes sometimes," said Winston, getting to his feet. "I'm going to get another sandwich. Anybody want anything?"

Todd turned to Elizabeth. "Are you going to finish those cookies, Liz?" he wanted to know. "Or should I get another dessert?"

"I really appreciate the lift," Jessica said as she got into Lila's Triumph after school on Tuesday. "I completely forgot that Liz was going to need the Jeep this afternoon."

"No problem," said Lila coolly, not even bothering to glance over at her. "After all, what are friends for?"

Jessica snapped her seat belt on, fighting the temptation to say that she was no longer sure what friends were for. It certainly didn't seem to her that they were for confiding in or telling your problems to. She glanced over at Lila, whose unmade-up skin looked pale and drawn. Today she was dressed in shapeless sweats, and even her hair looked dull. Just a few days ago Lila had been one of the most attractive girls in Southern California, but now she would have been lucky to come in as a runner-up in a Miss Organic-Egg beauty contest.

Jessica sighed, wondering how best to broach the subject of what might be wrong. The direct approach had failed miserably. Not that Jessica had been surprised, but Lila had never called her back yesterday afternoon, as she had promised. When Jessica finally telephoned Lila after dinner, she had talked about nothing but her English assignment and what had happened that afternoon on her favorite soap. "Lila," Jessica had said at last, "I'm really not interested in what's happening to Lance and Lana. I'm interested in what's happening to *you*." Lila had acted dumb. "I broke a nail playing volleyball, if that's what you mean," she had said.

Jessica turned to Lila with a smile as they pulled out of the parking lot. "So," she said. "Did I tell you Sam and I have finally decided to go to your costume ball as Princess Leia and Han Solo?" She made a face. "Thank goodness Sam thinks being a mercenary space pilot is almost as good as being a biker."

Lila, her eyes on the road, said, "That sounds great."

Jessica didn't let Lila's lack of enthusiasm stop her from going on. "Even Elizabeth and Todd have finally come up with something," she said. "Though it's very top secret. Liz won't even tell me what it is."

"Oh, no?" said Lila.

"No," said Jessica. She forced herself to laugh. "All I know for sure is that it isn't George and Martha Washington." She glanced over at Lila again, noticing how tightly she was holding the steering wheel. "So," she said, trying to make her voice sound light and casual, "have you finally decided what you're going as?"

Lila took the right-hand turn she was making so sharply that Jessica's bag fell to the floor. "To tell you the truth, I've been thinking of canceling the party," she suddenly blurted out.

Jessica put her bag back on her lap and turned to her friend with unconcealed amazement.

79

"You're *what*?" she squeaked. "Lila, you can't be serious! This is Tuesday. The ball's on Saturday. You *can't* change your mind now."

Swallowing hard, Lila swung the lime-green sports car into Calico Drive. "It's just that I'm so busy at the moment," she said shortly. "I just don't think I can handle a big party on top of everything else."

Hearing the frantic tone in Lila's voice, Jessica let her own voice show her concern. "On top of what else, Lila?" she asked. "What's going on?"

Lila pulled up in front of the Wakefield house. "Just everything," she said, keeping her eyes straight ahead of her and recovering her composure slightly. "I just have too much to do."

Impulsively, Jessica reached out and put a hand on Lila's shoulder. "Lila," she said gently. "Lila, I'm your best friend. If you've got some problem—"

"I told you," Lila interrupted, shaking off Jessica's hand. "I don't have a problem. I just have a lot to do, that's all."

Jessica opened the passenger door. "Sure," she said. "Whatever you say."

Jessica found it difficult to concentrate on anything that night. She barely tasted her dinner. She found herself reading the same paragraph in her history textbook over and over. She was almost glad that Sam's just-friends policy meant he didn't call her every night, since she wouldn't even have been able to concentrate on him. She

80

couldn't stop worrying about Lila. Every time she closed her eyes she saw Lila's profile in the car that afternoon, her lips tight, her eyes staring blankly at something in the distance. Finally, she decided to confide in her sister. Lila and Elizabeth had never been particularly friendly—in fact, they were usually particularly unfriendly—but she knew even that wouldn't stop her twin from being sympathetic.

Elizabeth listened to Jessica's story with a concerned expression on her face.

"I've tried everything I can to make her tell me what's wrong," Jessica finished. "But she just refuses to discuss it."

Elizabeth shook her head. "It must be something really major to throw Lila like this," she said. "I mean, Lila usually has *too* much self-confidence."

"That's why I'm so worried, Liz. I've never seen Lila like this. She couldn't be more unlike herself if she'd found out she was adopted and that she's being sent back to her real parents who are pig farmers in Nebraska."

Elizabeth laughed, but it was a serious laugh. "If it were something like that, she'd be angry," she said wisely. "This sounds more like depression."

Jessica flopped back on her sister's bed. "Lila Fowler, depressed! This is a first for medical science!" She turned to her twin. "What am I going to do, Liz? I want to help her, but she won't let me."

"You just have to keep trying," Elizabeth advised her. "You have to let her know that when she's ready to talk, you're ready to listen. There isn't anything else you can do."

Jessica propped herself on one elbow. "I don't really know if I should listen to you," she said, half joking. "Look where following your advice about Sam has gotten me."

Elizabeth threw a pillow at her sister. "Jessica," she said with a grin, "I told you to watch yourself, not lock yourself in a box."

# Six

In Lila's experience, when things went wrong, they soon got better. Her father might get angry with her because she had spent too much money on clothes, but within a week or two he would hand her back her credit cards. A really gorgeous boy might lose interest in her, but right behind him would be another, begging her to go out. She and Jessica might have a gigantic fight over something or other, but before you knew it they would be best friends again.

This time, however, things weren't getting better. Monday had been horrible, but the days that had followed had been even worse. She had stopped wearing makeup and worrying about how pretty she looked. The last thing in the world she wanted was to look attractive, to encourage some boy to get the wrong idea. "Well, look at the way she dresses," people would say. "What did she expect?"

Every night Lila relived her date with John in her nightmares, waking with her heart pounding. Every day she struggled to pretend that nothing had happened and to overcome the feeling of shame that clung to her like a layer of pond scum. She knew that Jessica and her other friends were worried about her, but the longer she went without confiding in them, the harder it became to even think of telling them the truth. Her secret separated her from them as effectively as a barbed-wire fence.

No, things weren't getting better. They were getting worse. Lila woke on Friday morning with her stomach in knots. Even when she had told Jessica that she was thinking of canceling the costume ball, she had known, in her heart, that there was no way that she could. Everyone had been invited. The food had been ordered. The decorations had been chosen. The only way she could cancel the party would be if she moved to Europe the following day.

There was one thing, however, that she had to cancel, and that was John Pfeifer. Even though she kept telling herself that he wouldn't—he couldn't possibly—come, not after what had happened, she also knew that for her own sanity and peace of mind she had to *tell* him not to come. Formally and officially. Because that would be the final humiliation. John Pfeifer, in her house, eating her food, sitting on her furniture, smiling and talking as though he were her friend and not her enemy. And Lila also knew that until she had said her piece to John he would continue to look at her as though he had gotten away with something.

Lila forced herself to get out of bed. She washed her face, put on the same baggy trousers and sweat shirt she had worn the day before, and ran a brush through her hair. She gazed at herself in the bathroom mirror. For the first time all week, she saw a determination, a spark of her old self in her face. "I'm going to tell him," she said to her reflection. "I'm going to tell him he can't come into my house under any circumstances. And then maybe everything really will be all right."

"How about if I give you a ride home today?" Lila asked Jessica as they left their last class together.

Jessica, not hiding her surprise, looked at her closely.

Lila rearranged her books in her arms. She had given it a lot of thought and had finally decided that she needed the moral support of just knowing that Jessica would be outside in the car waiting for her when she finished talking to John. "I've got a few more things to pick up for tomorrow night," she said, "and I thought maybe you could help me."

"You did?" asked Jessica.

Lila nodded, finally looking her friend in the

eyes. "Yes," she said. "I did. Then we could stop for a soda or something." She took a deep breath, suddenly realizing how much she had been missing Jessica. "It seems like a long time since we hung out together," she added in almost a whisper. Lila was half afraid that Jessica was going to tell her to take her ride and drop it in the ocean.

Instead, after a moment's hesitation, Jessica smiled. "Sure," she said. "That'd be great."

Lila sighed with relief. "Here," she said, handing Jessica the keys to the Triumph. "I have to see my math teacher about making up some homework. I'll meet you in the car."

Again that puzzled expression clouded Jessica's face. "You sure you don't want me to come with you?" she asked, the keys jangling in her hand.

"I'm sure," said Lila quickly. "This won't take long."


Lila knew that John was using the *Oracle* office on Friday afternoons to write his internship assignments. There was usually no one else there at that time, which meant that it was also the perfect place for her confrontation with him. Jamming her fists into the pockets of her sweat shirt, she marched down the corridor, going over what she would say in her head. All she wanted was to be able to tell him what she felt as calmly and coolly as possible. She didn't want him to see how upset she was. And she especially didn't want him to see her cry. She didn't want to lose her dignity in front of him; it was the only weapon she had against his contempt.

Lila hesitated at the door to the office, then pushed it open and walked in without knocking. *Be firm*, she told herself. *Don't let him talk you down.*

John, his back to her, was sitting at a corner desk, deep in thought. He must have thought it was Penny, or Elizabeth, or one of the other staff members coming in for something, because he didn't turn around.

"John." Lila was surprised to hear her own voice ring out so strongly in the quiet room. "John, there's something I want to say to you."

He looked up then. It was obvious from the startled expression on his face that she was the last person on earth he'd been expecting.

Holding onto her anger, Lila didn't wait for him to speak. "It's about tomorrow night," she said. "I'm assuming you wouldn't be insensitive enough to think that you were still invited to my party. But then I also assumed that you were a decent human being, and I wouldn't want to make the mistake of overestimating you again." Though her heart was pounding, she found that the more she talked, the easier it was. The words just seemed to pour out by themselves. "So, just so we're clear about it, John, let me make sure you understand that you are not welcome in my home. Not tomorrow; not ever."

She'd been afraid that he might argue with her, or pretend that he didn't understand what she was talking about, but instead he just shrugged. "Sure," he said. "If that's the way you want it, Lila."

"That's the way I want it."

"Whatever you say," he drawled. A smile flickered at the corners of his mouth. "You're the boss."

The minute Jessica saw Lila emerge from the school, her head held high, her face grim, she knew that Lila hadn't been to see her math teacher. Whatever business she had had to take care of was a lot more serious than making up a homework assignment.

"So, you get your homework all right?" she asked brightly as Lila slipped into the driver's seat.

Lila mumbled something Jessica took to be "yes." She glanced over at her and frowned. Not only did Lila look close to tears, but she was trembling so much that the keys Jessica handed her fell to the floor.

Lila sat there, looking at the keys glinting up at her from the Triumph's carpeted interior. *What is going on?* Jessica wondered as she bent down to retrieve them for her.

"Lila," she said as she handed her the gold chain and their fingers touched, "Lila, please tell me what's wrong. I'm your best friend. I want to help you."

Lila turned and looked her in the eyes for the first time all week. Jessica had never seen so much unhappiness in anyone's face before. For an instant, Lila seemed to be frozen, just sitting there staring at her, and then all at once she burst into tears.

"Oh, Jess!" she wailed. She buried her face in her hands and leaned her head on the steering wheel.

Jessica put an arm around her. "Lila, please. Tell me what's going on. Maybe I can help you . . ."

Lila shook her head. "I can't," she gasped. "I just can't. There isn't anything you can do. There isn't anything anyone can do."

"At least let me drive," said Jessica gently. "You're in no condition for that right now. At least let me drive until you calm down."

Lila didn't resist. Without a word of protest, she changed seats with Jessica and handed her back the keys. All the way home, Lila sat looking out the side window, the tears trickling down her cheeks, her mind a million miles away.

*Or maybe not a million miles away*, Jessica decided as she headed the lime-green Triumph toward Fowler Crest. *Maybe her thoughts aren't any further away than last Saturday night.* Jessica couldn't come up with any other explanation for the state Lila was in. Before the date she'd been her usual self; after it, she had been withdrawn and evasive. What else could it be?

She glanced over at Lila, folding and unfolding her hands on her lap, her eyes still glassy with tears. Jessica had been on bad dates before. Dates where he dumped his drink on her dress in the first ten minutes and then spent the next four hours telling her about the sleeping habits of salamanders. Dates where neither of them could think of anything to say. Dates where he fell asleep in the movie and started to snore. But nothing that would have caused her to react the way Lila had. Jessica scowled as she steered the Triumph through traffic. What in the world could have happened on one date to cause so much pain?

Lila moved her toy dagger out of the way and reached across the table to move the crudités and dip over half an inch. In the end, she had left selecting her own costume for so long that she had wound up having to choose between a mermaid and Peter Pan. Since she was definitely not feeling like a mermaid, she had taken Peter Pan.

"For heaven's sake, Lila," said Eva with an exasperated laugh. "Stop fiddling with everything, will you? Anybody would think you'd never had a party before."

Lila stepped back as Eva put another tray of sandwiches on the dining room table, where the rest of the food for the masquerade ball was already laid out. "I just want everything to be perfect," said Lila, trying not to sound as nervous as she felt.

Eva gave her a searching look. "You're acting like you're crossing the Sahara in your bare feet," said Eva. "Your guests are going to be arriving soon. Why don't you try to relax and leave me to finish getting things ready."

Lila straightened her hat on her head. "I guess I'll go sort through the CDs," she said.

Eva gave her a gentle shove in the direction of the door. "That's a great idea. You put on some music. That should calm you down."

The living room had been hung with purple balloons and large silver stars made out of paper. Miniature white Christmas-tree lights had been strung from wall to wall. Lila crossed to the stereo system and put on one of her favorite groups. She hoped that Eva was right, that music would make her feel calmer, but she wasn't so sure. She had made it through the week—not well, maybe, but she made it. If she could make it through this, the biggest party she had ever thrown, then she knew she would be all right. Tonight she would be surrounded by her friends. They would be talking and laughing and having fun. Everything would be normal. There would be no John Pfeifer skulking on the sidelines, reminding her of what had happened just a week ago that night. If she could have a good time herself, then she would know that she had been right not to say anything, that everything could go on as though nothing had ever occurred to disturb it. She might have a dreadful secret to cart around with her for the rest of her life, but at least it would be a secret. No one else would ever know how ashamed it made her feel.

Lila was jolted out of her thoughts by the doorbell. "I'll get it!" she called to Eva. She took a deep breath and glanced at herself in the mirror over the mantel. She was dressed as a twelve-year-old boy, but she looked more like herself than she had all week. Giving herself a smile of encouragement, she went to answer the door.

Because of Lila's breakdown the previous afternoon, Jessica had been worried about tonight's party. She had even thought that maybe she should have let Lila cancel it. Now, however, she was glad that it was taking place as planned. Not only did Lila seem to be more like her regular self than Jessica had seen her in the past week, but everyone else was having a great time as well. And the costumes! People had really outdone themselves. Jessica had thought that she and Sam were pretty terrific as Princess Leia and Han Solo, but she had to admit that there was some stiff competition. Just among their friends, Hugh had come as the body of a telephone and Enid as the receiver because of all the time they spent talking to each other on one, and Elizabeth and Todd were dressed as the sun and the moon, or day and night as Elizabeth had joked.

Sam put his arm around her and kissed the top of her head. "Having a good time?" he whispered.

Jessica nodded. The nicest part of masquerading as someone else was how comfortable she felt now with Sam. Maybe Jessica Wakefield had to be careful around him, but Princess Leia had no such problems with Han.

The sun, dancing with the moon, suddenly gave her a poke in the ribs. "Hey," teased Elizabeth, "I thought you two were from the first movie, where everyone thinks Princess Leia is going to end up with Luke."

"And I thought the sun and the moon usually kept more distance between each other," Jessica replied.

Some of Lila's old confidence began to return as the party really got under way, and the music and happy chatter pushed her sadder thoughts aside. How could she be miserable when the living room had been transformed into a magical world filled with ballet dancers and acrobats, with bears, and cats, and grinning clowns? Watching Princess Leia and Han Solo as they danced beside the sun and the moon, Lila had to smile. She was really glad now that she hadn't canceled the ball after all. Here she was serving cups of punch to a World War I fighter pilot and Raggedy Ann while they argued about which local high-school football team was the best. If she had canceled she would have been sitting by herself in her room right now, feeling like she didn't have a friend left in the world.

Lila looked toward the doorway as a new couple entered. He was dressed as a pirate and she was dressed as a fuzzy blue bunny. Lila watched them as they walked toward her, trying to figure out who they could be. She had the feeling that the bunny was a sophomore she knew only by sight, and whom she certainly hadn't invited, but the pirate was so well-masked by a beard, a mustache, and a jet-black eye patch that even though there was something familiar about him— something about the way he walked, something about the look he was giving his date—she couldn't tell who it was.

Lila put on her best hostess smile as the pirate, leaving the rabbit giggling a few feet away, approached her. Leaning on the table, he gave her a wicked wink. "Two glasses of punch, please, Lila," he said smoothly.

Lila, just about to lift the ladle out of the bowl, stopped in midair. John! The mysterious pirate was none other than John Pfeifer! Was he insane, coming here like this? Taunting her with his presence after she had told him he wasn't welcome? Her home was the one place she had felt safe from him, and now that safety had been violated.

Realizing that she had recognized him, his grin widened.

She dropped the ladle back into the punch with a splash. "I can't believe you," she hissed. "I can't believe you're this crazy." She dug her nails into her palms to stop herself from shaking. "If you don't get out of here, I'll have you thrown out!" she warned him. "I mean it, John. Don't think I don't."

He leaned nearer, smiling even more. "Really, Lila?" he asked. "Why? What reason will you give anyone? Because you're Peter Pan and you think I'm Captain Hook?" And with that he turned back to his bunny, putting his arm around her bright blue shoulder and pulling her close.

94

*　　*　　*

Lila watched John walk away. *How dare he defy me like this!* she fumed to herself. Wasn't it enough that she hadn't said a word to anyone? Wasn't it enough that he had scared her out of her mind? That he'd made her feel like dirt?

"Talk about adding insult to injury," Lila muttered, finding herself moving out from behind the punch bowl and toward the other side of the room, where the pirate and the rabbit were deep in conversation, without thinking about what she was doing.

At that moment all she could think of was how furious she felt. The one emotion all week long that Lila had not felt was pure, unadulterated rage. She'd been confused, ashamed, humiliated, and hurt, but any anger she had felt had turned on herself. Now all the anger was turned on John. She watched him flirting with the girl in the rabbit suit, smiling at her with all his charm, and she wanted to pull him away from her by force. She heard him laugh and she wanted to march right over there and hit him over the head with one of her father's priceless vases.

John, glancing over to where Lila stood, her eyes on him, said in a loud voice, "Why don't we get out of here now, Julie? This party is boring." He slipped an arm around her waist. "Let's go somewhere where we can be alone."

Lila felt something explode within her. It was as though all through this horrible week she had been under some sort of spell. As though she had been turned to stone. As though she had been waiting for someone to say the magic words to release her. And John had just said them. *Why don't we get out of here? Let's go somewhere where we can be alone.*

"No!" Lila screamed, stepping forward. "Don't go with him!"

She was dimly aware that Jessica had come up beside her. "Lila!" she whispered.

Lila shook her off, crossing the few feet that separated her from John and his date like a torpedo. Ignoring John's smiling face, she looked straight into the girl's wide gray eyes. "Listen to me," she said, her voice urgent with emotion. "Don't leave with him. Don't let him take you home."

The girl was visibly startled. Her eyes moved from Lila to John and back again.

Lila was aware that the room had become silent except for the background sound of the stereo. She could feel every eye on her, expectant and tense. "I mean it," Lila went on. "You'll be sorry if you leave with him. Take it from me."

The girl's eyes darted from Lila to John again. "I don't know what you mean," she said, her voice unsteady. "John?"

"Don't listen to her," said John coolly. "She's just jealous, that's all."

Lila felt rather than saw Sam and Todd each come up on one side of her. She could hear Sam saying something to her, something comforting and reassuring, but she wasn't listening. All at once the words were rushing out of her.

"Tell her!" she screamed, pointing at John. "Tell her why she shouldn't go with you. Tell her how you tried to rape me last Saturday night!"

Someone turned the CD player off.

Sam moved closer, his arm touching hers.

"Tell her!" Lila screamed again, tears suddenly streaming down her face, her body shaking uncontrollably. "Tell her what going someplace alone with you is like!"

John continued to look back at her with the calmness of a snake watching its supper draw near. "I don't know what you're talking about, Lila," he said in a voice full of bravado. He smiled patiently. "We both know what happened last Saturday, and it wasn't rape. In fact, it was anything but."

A murmur of whispers began to buzz through the room.

Lila opened her mouth to tell everyone what a liar he was, but her voice wouldn't work. It had taken every ounce of strength in her to say what she had, but he still stood there, confidently, sure of himself, lying through a smile.

Sam stepped in front of her. "I think you'd better get out of here, John," he said coldly. "If you know what's good for you."

"You mean if *you* know what's good for *her*," said John.

Lila turned and ran from the room. The front door slammed as she raced up the stairs.

# Seven

*"Tell her!"* screamed Lila. *"Tell her how you tried to rape me last Saturday night!"*

Jessica opened her eyes, the image of Lila's tear-stained face before her, and Lila's voice still ringing in her ears. She had tossed and turned for hours last night, going over what had happened at the party, before she finally fell into a restless, dream-haunted sleep.

Pushing back the covers, Jessica got out of bed with a sigh. Although it was still early, she knew there was no use in trying to go back to sleep. That morning, she was a girl with a mission, and she wouldn't rest until that mission was accomplished.

After Lila fled the party last night, Jessica had followed her upstairs. She stood outside Lila's locked bedroom door, knocking and calling, but Lila wouldn't let her in. "Go away!" Lila sobbed. "Just leave me alone, Jessica! Go away!" In the end, Jessica had gone away, but she certainly had no intention of staying away. Lila needed her, and Jessica was going to help her, whether her friend wanted her to or not.

Before she took her shower, Jessica called Lila. Eva said that Lila was still asleep.

After she took her shower, Jessica called Lila again. "I'm afraid she's still asleep, Jessica," said Eva.

Too preoccupied to eat, Jessica spent some time straightening up her room, to give herself something to do. While she stuffed things in drawers and shoved things under her bed, her mind was busy thinking of Lila and what she must have gone through between her date with John and the scene at the costume ball. No wonder Lila had seemed so distant and unhappy all week. No wonder Jessica hadn't been able to guess what had happened to upset her friend so much! Who could have dreamed of such a thing? Seven whole days of keeping that horrible secret to herself!

Elizabeth came into her room just as Jessica was hanging up the phone.

"Were you talking to Lila?" asked Elizabeth.

Jessica shook her head. "No, I was talking to Eva for the third time this morning." She made a face. "Lila refuses to come to the phone."

"I guess that's understandable," said Elizabeth,

sitting down on the foot of her sister's bed. "She probably needs to be alone for a while."

"Are you kidding?" asked Jessica. She started putting on her sneakers. "Lila's been alone since the whole thing happened. What she needs now is to know that she's *not* alone."

Elizabeth looked doubtful. "Jessica, this is a really difficult situation, you know. I'm not sure you should go marching in like you usually do. Maybe you should use a little tact and discretion for a change."

Jessica stood up, reaching for her sweater and her shoulder bag. "Don't talk to me about tact and discretion," she snapped. "Talk to your friend John Pfeifer about them!"

After Jessica stormed out of the house, Elizabeth walked over to the window, lost in thought, her sister's words echoing in her head. Everyone at the party had been shocked by the scene between Lila and John, but no one more than Elizabeth herself. John Pfeifer had been her friend for a long time. She couldn't understand how he could have done what Lila accused him of doing. John? He was intense, Elizabeth knew that about him, and sometimes he struck her as *too* intense. She thought about how he had acted when he was trying to get Jennifer Mitchell to break up with Rick Andover. Even though she had agreed that he was right, she hadn't approved of his methods. "Strong-arm tactics," she had thought of them as at the time.

Elizabeth watched as the Jeep slowly backed out of the driveway. What was it Jessica had said about Jennifer Mitchell? She frowned, trying to remember the conversation. Then it came back to her. Jennifer had told Jessica that the reason she broke up with John was because he was so bossy and overbearing. "She says he just doesn't know when to stop," Jessica had told her. Elizabeth had laughed. "Well, I guess he is a little pigheaded," she had said. "It's part of his charm."

*Maybe charm wasn't the right word for it*, Elizabeth thought as she headed downstairs. Another conversation came back to her. The conversation she had overheard inside the *Oracle* office the other day. John Pfeifer saying, "Well, you know what girls are like. They never know what they want. They tell you one thing, and then they get mad at you when that's what you do."

The memory of Lila as she had been last night came back to her. She had overheard someone say that Lila was exaggerating. Someone else said Lila was probably making it up. Elizabeth couldn't imagine how anyone could have made up the look on Lila's face, or the anguish in her voice. Just the memory caused a chill to run through Elizabeth. On the other hand, though, she couldn't condemn John without any evidence. How could she, when she still believed that the boy she knew—the boy she had worked with and confided in all these years—would never have done such a thing, not in a million years?

"What's the matter, Liz?" asked Mrs. Wakefield as her daughter came into the kitchen. "You look like you've lost your best friend."

Elizabeth sat down across from her mother. "Not quite," she said with a grim smile. "I think it might actually be worse."

Mrs. Wakefield put down the piece of toast she had been about to bite into. "Why, Elizabeth," she said in concern. "What's happened?"

Elizabeth hadn't really planned to tell her mother about Lila and John, but she was so confused in her own mind that it suddenly seemed like the right thing to do. "I really don't know how to begin," she said slowly. "But the most awful thing has happened, Mom, and I just don't understand it. It doesn't even seem possible . . ."

Mrs. Wakefield listened to Elizabeth's story in complete silence. Only when Elizabeth was done did she speak. "You never think it could be someone you know," Mrs. Wakefield said. "When we hear stories about things like this, we always think the boy must be either a criminal or a monster." She shook her head sadly. "Not a nice boy like John."

Elizabeth ran a hand through her hair. "That's just what I mean. How could someone I know, someone I've always liked and trusted, *do* a thing like this? It just doesn't make sense." She pushed her breakfast away. "On the other hand, though, I can't believe Lila would invent this whole thing. I mean, why? And if you had seen her face . . ."

"A thing like this doesn't make sense," said

Mrs. Wakefield, choosing her words carefully. "I don't even think there's any way anyone could have predicted it would happen. I'm sure that if what Lila says is true, John didn't ask Lila out thinking that that was how the evening would end."

"Poor Lila." Elizabeth sighed. "This past week must have been a nightmare for her."

A worried frown appeared on Mrs. Wakefield's face. "Let's just hope this is the end of the nightmare and not the beginning," she said softly.

Elizabeth looked at her sharply. "What do you mean?" she demanded.

"Nothing's been proven, has it, Elizabeth?" Elizabeth shook her head. "I know Jessica won't have a doubt in her mind about what Lila's said," Mrs. Wakefield continued. "And I know that even though you feel you have to give John the benefit of the doubt so long as there is no proof, you'll still be sympathetic to Lila. But not everyone might be, Liz. After all, John is a very respected young man. There are bound to be rumors. There are bound to be people who think that even if something did happen, it's Lila's fault."

"Lila's fault?" Elizabeth stared at her mother in disbelief. "But how could it be Lila's fault?"

Mrs. Wakefield lifted her coffee cup to her lips. "And how could a nice boy like John do something like that?" she asked.

\*　　\*　　\*

As soon as Eva answered the door, Jessica held up her hand. "Don't tell me," she said. "I already know. Lila's not up yet."

Eva, who had opened her mouth to speak, closed it again and stepped back as Jessica strode past her into the hallway and started toward the stairs.

Jessica half expected to discover that Lila had locked her bedroom door, but when she turned the knob, the door opened.

"I already told you, Eva," said Lila's muffled voice. "I don't want to see anyone. Tell whoever it is that I'm still asleep."

"You can tell me yourself," said Jessica, gently shutting the door behind her.

Lila was sitting on the bed, her arms around the teddy bear she had slept with when she was a child. She looked like a ghost. Her skin was pale from lack of sleep, her hair was uncombed, and her eyes were red from weeping. "Oh, Jessica," she whispered, "it's been so horrible . . ."

At the sight of Lila, all the wise and practical things Jessica had planned to say vanished from her mind. Without another word she ran over and threw her arms around her friend.

Haltingly, and through her tears, Lila told Jessica every painful detail of what had happened on her date with John.

"Why didn't you tell me before?" asked Jessica when Lila was finally through. "Why didn't you let me help you?"

Lila shook her head. "I felt . . . I don't know, I guess I just felt so confused," she stammered. "I was so ashamed, Jess. I know this doesn't really make any sense, but I kept thinking that it must be my fault somehow. That if I told anyone they'd say I'd asked for it."

"It's like that article Elizabeth wrote on sexual harassment, isn't it?" asked Jessica, remembering all the trouble her twin had had getting the piece published in the first place. "Part of her point was that girls are afraid to speak up because they think no one will believe them, or that if someone comes on to them it's their fault somehow."

"I know that," Lila answered quickly. "I was on her side, if you remember."

"Yeah, but don't you see?" Jessica persisted. "This isn't any different."

Lila bit her lip.

Jessica went on. "Instead of being angry and thinking you had a right to stand up for yourself, you took all the blame."

"I guess you're right, Jess," said Lila. "It wasn't until last night, when he came to my house after I'd told him not to, that I stopped feeling guilty and started feeling mad. And then, when I thought he might do the same thing to the girl he was with . . . Well, suddenly I realized that I'd been wrong. That everything wasn't all right just because I pretended that it was."

Jessica's blue-green eyes blazed with fury. "You just wait till we get through telling everybody about John Pfeifer," she said. "He won't be able to hold his head up in Sweet Valley High after this."

Lila made a face. "Let's just hope that *I* can," she said.

Jessica took the long way back home. She wanted time to think over everything Lila told her, in particular the events leading up to that awful Saturday night. How nice the first part of Lila's date with John had been. How it was she who suggested they go up to Miller's Point. How much she had liked kissing him. "That's why I thought that maybe the whole thing was my fault," Lila had confided. "Because I enjoyed it so much. He said I'd led him on. He said I'd asked for it."

Jessica couldn't help thinking about Sam. What would have happened if Sam weren't the wonderful boy he was, but someone like John Pfeifer? "But he isn't like John Pfeifer," she said aloud, answering her own question. "He's Sam Woodruff." A warm, safe feeling came over Jessica. Sam thought she was the prettiest girl he had ever known. He liked to hug her and kiss her, just as much as she liked to hug and kiss him. But more than that, Sam loved and respected her. Sam would never do anything to hurt her or cause her pain. Just as she would never do anything to hurt him. For the first time all day, an enormous smile lit up Jessica's face. She could kiss Sam Woodruff till her lips got chapped, and what had happened to Lila on Miller's Point would never happen to her. Because Sam wasn't anything like John Pfeifer. Sam could be trusted. Sam cared about her. Which was what Sam had been trying to tell her all along, of course. That they were safe with each other.

Jessica turned the Jeep into Calico Drive. Her heart skipped a beat when she saw Sam's car parked in front of her house. As she pulled into the driveway, Sam came out the back door.

"What are you doing here?" asked Jessica.

Sam leaned against the side of the car. "I figured you'd go to Lila's first thing, so I thought I'd be here when you came back." The smile he gave her was a serious one. "You know," he went on, "in case you needed to talk to me."

Jessica climbed down from the Jeep. She knew exactly what she needed to do. She needed to kiss Sam Woodruff as hard as she could.

"All this stuff with John . . ." Sam was saying. "I wanted you to know I've been thinking about it, and I know what you've been afraid of with us."

Jessica moved a little closer to him. "I—"

Sam cut her off. "No, let me finish, Jess. I know what you've been afraid of, but you've got to believe me when I say that I wouldn't jeopardize what we have for anything."

"I wouldn't either," said Jessica, fighting back a smile.

Sam sighed. "So if you really think we should cool it, well—"

It was Jessica's turn to cut him off. "Cool it?" she asked, slipping her arms around him. "Why would I want to cool it when I have the most wonderful boyfriend a girl could ask for?"

Sam looked at her in delighted surprise. "You mean this hasn't turned you against boys once and for all?"

Jessica shook her head. "It's turned me against John Pfeifer once and for all," she said, leaning against him. "But as far as you're concerned, Mr. Woodruff, it's made me realize how lucky I am. When I think of what Lila went through . . ."

Sam held her tight. "You just tell Lila that if there's anything I can do to help—like dump Pfeifer in the Pacific—all she has to do is ask."

"All you have to do right now is kiss me," Jessica said softly.

Sam grinned. "Here? In broad daylight?"

She gave him a poke. "No, you dope." Jessica raised her lips to his. "Here on my mouth."


"You have to admit one thing," said Todd as he and Elizabeth slid into a booth in the Dairi Burger on Sunday afternoon. "Going as day and night was a pretty inspired idea, as things turned out."

"I guess you're right," said Elizabeth with a sigh. "There are times when it doesn't seem like the two sexes have much in common."

Todd reached for her hand across the table. "Oh, I don't know about that," he said earnestly. "But there can be a difference between the way guys think and the way girls do." He squeezed her hand. "It's what I was trying to tell you before, Liz."

Elizabeth frowned. "You mean about Arthur Castillo?"

"I'm not saying your prince is like John," Todd said quickly. "I'm just saying that you can't always take things for granted."

"I never thought *John* was like John," Elizabeth said with a shake of her head. "And we don't really know that he is, do we? I mean, it's not that in my heart I don't believe Lila, but it *is* still just her word against his. I mean, Jessica said that Jennifer broke up with John because he was being bossy and overbearing, but I've never really seen that side of him."

Todd shrugged. "People are full of surprises, you know."

Elizabeth gave him a kick under the table. "Yes, I know," she said. "Even you."

Todd flushed. "Are we talking about your prince again?"

"Are you trying to tell me that you weren't a little jealous?"

Todd laughed. "No," he grinned. "I'm not trying to tell you that."

"You sure you don't want us to give you a lift to school tomorrow?" asked Jessica, twirling the phone cord in her left hand. "I thought you might want some extra moral support."

"It's OK, Jess," Lila answered. Since her talk

with Jessica earlier in the day, she was feeling much stronger and clearer. Everything was going to be all right after all. Not because she was pretending that nothing had happened, but because she had finally admitted what had. "Just having you in my corner is enough," she said sincerely. She paused for a second, staring at the phone, and then she went on in a voice that was low with emotion. "I can't tell you what a difference talking to you has made for me. I wish I hadn't been so frightened of telling you before."

Jessica's warm, affectionate laugh bounced down the line. "Just don't let it happen again, all right?"

"All right," said Lila, laughing herself. "I'll see you at school."

She hung up the phone and began to get ready for bed, feeling almost happy. It wasn't just the relief of having Jessica to lean on that was making her feel so much better, it was the relief of having it all out in the open. Just the act of confronting John at last had made her feel stronger and clearer.

*Jessica's right*, she thought as she climbed under the covers. *Now that the truth is out, John Pfeifer won't be able to hold up his head.*

# Eight

Jessica sailed into the kitchen on Monday morning, humming an upbeat tune. She was dressed in a kaleidoscope of bright colors, and large gold hoops dangled from her ears.

"Well, look at you!" cried Mrs. Wakefield with a smile. "You look like you're going to a party, not to school."

Jessica smiled back. "I'm celebrating," she said as she took her place at the table. Although she hadn't spoken to her mother about it herself, she knew that Elizabeth had told Mrs. Wakefield what had happened to Lila. "I'm so happy that everything's going to be all right for Lila that I want the world to know it."

Elizabeth caught her sister's eye. "You don't think maybe you're being a little premature,

Jess?" she asked gently. "I mean, Lila might still have a hard time, you know."

Jessica looked from her sister to her mother. Both of them were watching her with worried expressions on their faces. "What are you talking about?" She helped herself to a slice of toast. "Everything's out in the open now. Once everybody in school hears how John behaved, he won't have a friend left."

Mrs. Wakefield pursed her lips. "I wouldn't be so sure of that," she said slowly. "There are two sides to every story, remember. Some people are going to believe John."

"Mom's right," Elizabeth agreed quickly. "I mean, I know Lila's telling the truth, Jessica, but I still have a hard time believing that my friend John did something like that. It's like Dr. Pfeifer and Mr. Hyde. Anyway, there's no way of *proving* what really did go on, is there?"

Jessica's eyes darkened. "I don't believe I'm hearing this!" She dropped her knife onto her plate with a clang. "You two are the ones who are always telling me that honesty is the best policy. You're the ones who always say that the truth will win in the end."

"And we're still saying that," Mrs. Wakefield assured her.

Elizabeth shook her head. "We're just saying that it might take a little longer for it to win than you think."

For the first time since her date with John, Lila got up on Monday looking forward to the day ahead. She dressed with care, choosing one of her favorite outfits and tying her hair with a matching scarf. She carefully applied her makeup, taking longer in front of the bathroom mirror on that one morning than she had on all the mornings of the previous week put together. When she was done, Lila stepped back to check the effect, just as she used to do. She smiled at her reflection. Before, when she had looked into the mirror, the girl staring back at her had seemed only half alive, the Sweet Valley High zombie, but not anymore. Today she looked nice. Pretty. Normal.

Lila swung her bag over her shoulder as she left the house and walked toward the Triumph. It really did look like everything was going to be all right.

By the time she had parked her car and entered the high school, Lila was beginning to wish that she had taken Jessica up on her offer of a ride to school. She could have used a little moral support after all. Students stepped back as she approached. Some of them looked away, but some of them watched her with open curiosity.

Lila tried to ignore the looks and whispers that followed her as she walked down the corridor toward her locker. Twenty minutes ago she had thought the world was her oyster again, and now here it was, looking like an empty shell.

Lila tried to hold her head up high as she marched down the hall. She didn't have to be Sherlock Holmes to realize that news of the scene between her and John at the costume ball had spread through the student body. The school day hadn't even begun, but already the rumors and stories were flying. And it was obvious to her that not everyone believed her story.

Lila turned toward her locker and nearly walked into John. He was standing with a group of his friends outside the *Oracle* office. Lila couldn't disguise her surprise. She and Jessica had thought that John Pfeifer wouldn't be able to hold up his head after her revelation on Saturday night, but he was having no trouble holding up his head. No trouble smiling. No trouble laughing. No trouble acting as though nothing had happened; as though he were one of the nicest guys Sweet Valley High had ever seen.

Meeting her eyes, John's expression changed from good-humored and boyish to coldly arrogant. An insolent smirk turned up the corners of his mouth. Lila forced herself to look back at him with a defiance of her own, but she could feel her heart pound. He wasn't sorry. He wasn't ashamed. He looked, in fact, like a boy who knows that he is completely in the right. John nudged one of his friends and mumbled something out of the corner of his mouth. The other boys began to laugh, watching Lila out of the corner of their eyes.

Her cheeks burning, Lila sped past them as fast as she could.

*　　*　　*

Jessica was thinking about John Pfeifer as she changed back into her regular clothes after gym. She was thinking that she would like to bring back tar and feathering and practice on him. "The nerve of him," Jessica muttered to herself as she pulled on her leggings.

Because she and Elizabeth had some trouble with the Jeep that morning they were late getting to school, and she missed seeing Lila completely. But she had run into John Pfeifer. She was just hurrying to her homeroom when he suddenly appeared in the hall. She would have thought that he would skulk past her as quickly as he could, but instead he stopped and gave her a big hello. Jessica froze, half in outrage and half in surprise.

"If you see Elizabeth, tell her I'd like to meet her later in the office," John told her with a grin. "I have an idea for the next issue of *The Oracle* that I want to run by her."

Before Jessica could respond, he had turned and gone on his way, leaving her staring after him.

As she was putting on her shoes and thinking of the sarcastic comebacks she should have made, she heard her best friend's name mentioned.

"Did you hear what happened at Lila Fowler's party Saturday night?" asked a voice on the other side of the lockers.

Jessica opened her ears.

"You mean with John Pfeifer?" came the reply.

"That's right," said the first girl. "Can you believe it? I mean, I don't know John personally, but he's always seemed like such a nice guy. You know, steady and serious."

The other girl banged her locker shut. "Yeah, but we've only heard *her* side of the story." She laughed. "After all, you do have to consider the source. You know the sort of reputation she has as well as I do."

Everything her sister and her mother had said that morning came back to Jessica in a furious rush. Maybe they had been more right about the sort of reaction Lila could expect than Jessica had been willing to accept.

Without an instant's hesitation, Jessica was on her feet and around the side of the lockers, still holding one of her shoes in her hand. "Just what are you trying to say!" she demanded. "Are you suggesting that Lila's lying?"

Stunned, the two girls just stared at her for a second, but then the second girl recovered herself. "Look," she said calmly, "I know Lila's your best friend and everything, Jessica, but you have to face the facts. Lila's a flirt. Everybody knows that." She shrugged. "She does everything she can to attract boys, so what does she expect?"

"She expects a little more understanding from other girls, that's what she expects," said Jessica contemptuously. She turned on her heel. "Not that it looks as though she's going to get it," she added as she stormed away.

\*   \*   \*

Elizabeth was having lunch that afternoon with Todd, Enid, Ken Matthews and Terri Adams. Terri and Enid were debating how many calories there were in the rice salad when Elizabeth noticed Lila and Jessica enter the cafeteria. Jessica, apparently oblivious to the looks Lila was attracting, waved to a few people she knew and went right over to the lunch line. Lila, however, stood in the doorway for a second, looking around in much the way that a deer coming from the woods into a clearing will stop and look around.

Enid followed her gaze. "Have you noticed how people are looking at her?" she asked in almost a whisper. She and Elizabeth had discussed what had happened on Saturday night, of course, and Enid agreed that there was no doubt in her mind that Lila was telling the truth.

Elizabeth nodded. "It's even worse than I was afraid it might be," she said somberly. "I can't tell you how many girls I've overheard saying that even if what Lila said was true she'd probably gotten what she asked for."

"Me, too," said Terri. She shook her head sadly. "I know as well as anyone that Lila isn't exactly Little Miss Innocence," she went on, "but you'd think people would realize that a girl wouldn't make an accusation like that just for the fun of it."

"Exactly," said Enid. She sighed. "I never thought I'd hear myself say this, but I feel really sorry for Lila. Everywhere she goes, people look

117

at her like she's a leper or something. All she has to do is walk into a room for everyone to stop talking completely."

Elizabeth picked up her sandwich, but put it right down again. Even though she had predicted this reaction, she had to admit that she was a little surprised by how rampant it was. "You'd think at least the girls would try to be understanding, wouldn't you?" she asked. She looked over at Todd and Terri. "What are the boys saying?" she wanted to know.

Todd glanced at her out of the corner of his eye. "I'm not so sure I should tell you," he half joked.

Elizabeth gave him a look. "If you say, 'You know what guys are like,' I'm going to hit you, Todd."

"But you do know what guys are like," cut in Ken. He shrugged apologetically. "I'm not defending them, Liz. I'm just saying what you already know. A lot of the boys are shocked by what Lila says happened. But a lot of them are saying that Lila knew what she was doing and now she's trying to make herself feel better by putting all the blame on John."

Todd nodded. "If you want the truth, Liz," he said, looking over at Ken for support, "John's telling everyone it was Lila's idea to go up to Miller's Point in the first place."

Enid, Elizabeth, and Terri exchanged a look.

Elizabeth raised her chin. "So what if it was?" she demanded. "It seems to me, Todd, that

118

there've been times when I've suggested we go somewhere where we can be alone."

"But not on the first date," said Ken. He raised his eyebrows. "I mean, you've got to admit it, girls. You can't really blame John for getting the wrong idea."

Terri scowled at him. "Ken Matthews!" she screamed. "I don't *believe* what I'm hearing. Are you saying that John had a right to attack Lila because it was her idea to go for a drive?"

Confused, Ken looked to Todd for help. Todd rolled his eyes. "Well ... um ... well, no ..." Ken stammered. "That's not what *I'm* saying. It's what the other guys are saying."

Todd put his arm around Elizabeth's chair. "Look," he said reasonably. "Let's not forget what happened when Kris Lynch spread those lies about you, Liz. People believed him, even though they know what you're like. Even though you don't play the field, or flirt, or dress to conquer like Lila does."

Elizabeth narrowed her eyes. "So now you're saying that Lila deserved what happened because she's popular and attractive and she doesn't dress in potato sacks?"

Todd rested his head in his hands. "I think we're digging a hole for ourselves here," he said to Ken.

"I'm just a little surprised that no one seems to be as critical of John as they are of Lila," said Elizabeth coolly.

Todd made a face. "Weren't you the one who

119

said yesterday that you couldn't believe that John would do a thing like that? Didn't you say he couldn't be hanged without a fair trial?"

Elizabeth stirred her milk with her straw. "Yes, I said that," she admitted. "But it wasn't because I doubted Lila. It was because John's my friend, and because there isn't any concrete evidence. But even so, I know what I saw in Lila's face . . ."

Todd spread his hands. "I rest my case," he said. "You can't blame others for being as confused as you admit you were, Liz. John has a reputation as a serious, hardworking, and responsible guy. I saw Lila's face on Saturday night and I'm sure she was telling the truth, too. But you can't deny that the only thing against him is Lila's word." He leaned over and kissed her on the ear. "Tell the truth," he teased. "You'd be the first to defend him if everyone turned against John on nothing but circumstantial evidence, and don't tell me you wouldn't."

Elizabeth grimaced, forced to acknowledge the truth of what he was saying.

"I guess the boys do have a point," said Enid.

Terri nodded. "It is just her word against his," she agreed.

Elizabeth picked up her crumpled napkin and threw it at Todd. "Sometimes it really annoys me when you're right," she said.

"Look at how people are staring at me," Lila whispered to Jessica as they crossed the cafeteria together. "I feel like I should be wearing a sign that says 'She Got What She Deserved.'"

Jessica tossed back her hair. "Don't be ridiculous," she said. "They're staring at you with admiration because you had the courage to stand up and tell the truth."

"Oh, please," said Lila with more of her old spirit than she had been feeling all day. "Don't try to protect me, Jess. I know what people are saying. A lot of them believe John."

Jessica, acting as though she hadn't heard Lila, put her tray down on the table where Amy and Caroline were already sitting. "Rice salad again," she said to the other girls. "There must have been a sale on peas and brown rice. It's all the cooks here ever seem to make anymore."

Lila dropped her own tray on the table and slumped into a chair. Although a few people had gone out of their way to show support for her, the general reaction seemed to be so much more in John's favor than hers that she was finding it hard to keep up her morale.

"I don't know how you can talk about rice at a time like this," she complained.

Amy touched her shoulder lightly. "Oh, come on, Lila," she coaxed. "Cheer up a little, will you? You've still got us."

"That's right," said Caroline. "And we're doing all we can to help you."

Jessica winked. "And when you've got Caroline on your team, you have one of the most efficient communication systems in the world," she joked.

Lila pushed her tray away. "Go on and joke about all this," she said, throwing her arms in the air. "But I knew this would happen. Everyone is blaming me for what John did."

Jessica shot her a meaningful look. "Not everyone," she said. "And you know it."

Lila leaned back in her seat. "I guess the trouble is that I almost agree with them," she confessed. "I mean, I was there, and sometimes I think it must have been my fault. It shouldn't upset me that other people think so, too."

Amy glanced at Jessica and Caroline. "Why don't you call the hotline, Lila?" she asked. "You'd be amazed how common this sort of reaction is. If you could talk to someone who understands what you're going through, I'm sure you'd feel better." She shook her head sadly. "This is exactly the reason so many girls don't speak out," she went on. "It's not just that they're afraid people will turn against them, they're afraid they might be right to."

Jessica pointed her fork at her friend. "Lila, for the millionth time, *you* didn't do anything wrong. Just because you kiss a boy doesn't mean he has the right to attack you. I mean, they're human, too, you know. They're supposed to act like it."

Caroline nodded. "Jess is right. It's not your fault, and blaming yourself is the last thing you should do." She fiddled with the wrapper on her sandwich. "You know, almost the same thing happened to a cousin of mine, Lila." She raised her eyes to her friends. "It was awful what she went through. Really awful." Caroline shuddered. "I almost feel like I went through it myself, only secondhand."

"Secondhand is the best way to go through it, if you ask me," said Lila sourly.

"I don't want to hear you talking like that, Lila Fowler," Jessica ordered, snapping a celery stick in two. "That's defeatist talk. We're into fighting here."

Lila smiled ruefully. "I guess I should be thankful that you're on my side," she said.

# Nine

"This is what the rest of my life is going to be like," said Lila glumly as she and Jessica walked down the hallway together on Tuesday morning. "Everyone's always going to be looking at me like I have an extra head."

Jessica glared at a group of girls who were whispering by the water fountain as they passed. "I still don't think you should take this lying down," she said with a toss of her head. "I think you should take this to the authorities. Write a letter to *The Oracle*. Make sure everyone knows your side of the story."

Lila bit her bottom lip. "And I think I should transfer to a private school where no one knows anything about me."

Jessica looked at her sharply. "That's a joke,

right? You're not really thinking of anything that drastic, are you?"

Lila shifted her books in her arms. The truth was that though she wasn't completely serious, she wasn't really joking, either. It wasn't just that she couldn't stand the looks and rumors and the knowledge that a lot of people thought she was the villain. It was that she couldn't imagine ever going out on a date again, not in Sweet Valley. What sort of boy would date her now? What boy could she ever trust?

"Lila," Jessica persisted. "Tell me you're not serious about going to a different school."

Lila tried to make her laugh sound light. "No, of course not," she said, shaking her head. "I'll just dye my hair red and move to Alaska."

On her way to lunch that afternoon, Jessica spotted Jennifer Mitchell going into the *Oracle* office. Up until now, Jennifer had managed to keep out of the controversy surrounding John and Lila, but as she watched the slim blond figure disappear through the door, Jessica couldn't help wondering if it wasn't about time that Jennifer got involved.

Impulsively, Jessica changed direction and turned to the right. Maybe she could find out something about John from Jennifer that supported Lila's accusation. If something didn't happen soon to vindicate Lila, she was going to start sliding back into the depression she had been in the previous week. Although she hadn't quite returned to wearing baggy sweats and walking around like she had to apologize for breathing, Jessica had noticed that Lila wasn't wearing much makeup today, and that her step had lost a lot of its bounce. If she didn't put a stop to this, Lila might just end up transferring to a different school.

Jessica's eyes darkened with determination as she reached the door to the newspaper office. Just because Lila drove her crazy sometimes didn't mean Jessica would want to live without her. Life in Sweet Valley would be incredibly dull without Lila Fowler around to keep her on her toes. Unless, of course, it was a Lila Fowler who had been so intimidated that she made Elizabeth Wakefield seem like a wild woman.

Jessica followed Jennifer into the office without even bothering to knock. "Jennifer?" she called, stopping just inside the door. "Do you have a minute?"

Jennifer was just putting her things down on a desk. She turned around. "Hi, Jess," she said, not showing any surprise. "What can I do for you?"

Jessica shut the door behind her. "I wanted to talk to you about John," she said.

Jennifer looked down at the floor for a second. "You mean about what Lila says happened up on Miller's Point?"

Jessica nodded. "I don't want to pry into what went on between you and John," she said quickly. "But I just thought that maybe, if there

126

was something that you could say to Lila ... she's having such a rough time."

With an unhappy smile, Jennifer slid onto the desk, her hands folded in her lap. "I wish I could help you, Jess," she said quietly. "I really do. I can't believe Lila would make up something like this. I mean, who would? You'd have to be completely demented to put yourself through what Lila's going through." She shook her head. "But I'm afraid that there isn't anything I can say. I already told you, John and I broke up because he always has to take control. Everything has to be done his way or not at all. But that has nothing to do with this other thing." She spread her hands in an empty gesture. "As far as I'm concerned, Jessica, I have no personal reason to believe that John might be capable of this."

"Don't you think, though, that maybe if you talked to him ... maybe you could convince him to go for help."

"I told you, Jess," Jennifer said gently. "I'm not completely convinced that he needs help. And even if he did, he wouldn't go because I asked him to. He won't do anything unless he wants to do it."

Jessica nodded. Deep down, she supposed, she had already known that this was what Jennifer would say. "Well, thanks," she said. "I really appreciate your directness."

Jennifer extended her hand. "Tell Lila I admire her bravery in speaking out like she did," she said.

"I don't know if Lila thinks it was bravery," said Jessica ruefully. "I think she thinks it was a huge mistake."

As she made her way through the lunch line, Lila was beginning to think that her outburst on Saturday night wasn't bravery and wasn't just a mistake, either. It was total insanity. She had been pushed over the edge by John Pfeifer's presence in her home, and as a result she had lost her mind. The problem was that it was still lost. She put a bowl of salad beside her sandwich and moved up to the cashier. If she didn't find it again she might have to make good on her threat to Jessica and really transfer to another school. An all-girls school somewhere so far away that no one there would ever have heard of her.

Lila paid for her lunch and picked up her tray. Although the Sweet Valley High cafeteria was no larger today than it was on any other day, as she turned to cross it to go to her table, Lila couldn't help feeling that it was about as wide across as the Pacific Ocean, and just as treacherous. Between her and the corner where Amy and Robin Wilson sat chatting happily were dozens of hostile faces, yards of space to cover where everyone would be looking at nothing but her. Ever since yesterday, Lila couldn't walk anywhere without feeling as though she were on a catwalk, spotlights on her and everyone waiting for her to fall.

*It's your imagination*, she told herself as she stared out at the rows of crowded tables. *Nobody's*

*looking at you. Nobody's talking about you. They're
eating their lunches. They're talking about their homework and the next basketball game.*

A little behind her, a boy laughed.

At her. What else could it be, but at her? Lila's
face went scarlet. Of course she had been right.
No one at Sweet Valley High had anything to
talk about but her anymore. Everywhere she
went, Lila Fowler was the only topic of conversation. Lila Fowler and how she dressed . . . how
she flirted . . . how she liked to kiss . . . how she
had led sincere, kind, serious John Pfeifer on and
then cried wolf . . .

"You better watch yourself," said a husky male
voice. "She's really hot."

Lila swung around, her face burning. Behind
her, Jimmy, the counterman, was watching the
new kitchen worker put another tray of potatoes
into place. He looked over and smiled at her
kindly. "You OK?" he asked.

Swallowing hard, Lila nodded. "Yes," she said,
hoping her voice didn't betray her. "Yes, I'm
fine." She turned back and started toward Amy
and Robin, blinking back a few tears.

*You're almost there,* she told herself as she
reached the halfway point. Amy was waving to
her and Robin was smiling. In a minute, she
would be sitting at the table with them, eating
her lunch with her friends just like anybody else.
In less than a minute; in only a few seconds.

All of a sudden, John Pfeifer was standing in
her path. Lila hadn't seen him sitting at a nearby

table, and she hadn't seen him get up and start toward the food line. But she saw him stop in the middle of the center aisle that ran the length of the cafeteria and just stand there looking at her. Lila forced herself to keep going. Now everyone really was looking at her. She could hear talk and laughter and the clanging and clicking of cutlery, but more than that she could hear a silence spreading. It was as though she were walking down the main street of Dodge City. Billy the Kid was waiting for her at the other end, only she didn't have a gun.

A slow smile appeared on John's face as Lila got closer. *He's going to talk to me!* she thought. *He's going to say something!* Two weeks ago, a lifetime away, Lila Fowler could have strode past the Prince of Wales with her head held high and a patronizing look in her eyes. Now she couldn't face an ordinary high school boy.

She could see him getting ready to speak. She could feel herself getting ready to turn and run. But all at once she wasn't alone. Out of nowhere, Elizabeth appeared on one side of her and Enid on the other.

"I can't believe it," Elizabeth was saying, as though they had been chatting together all along. "We never even thanked you for the party the other night. Considering how many sandwiches Todd put away, we should have written you a thank-you note."

Enid laughed. "Todd! I practically had to drag

Hugh away from the guacamole. I was sure he'd be green by the end of the evening."

Lila couldn't think of anything to say in reply, but then she didn't have to. She felt the girls' arms brush against hers as they strode past John Pfeifer as though he weren't even there.

"There was only one thing wrong with your party as far as I could tell," said Elizabeth in a clear, loud voice. "And that was the gatecrasher."

"Yeah," agreed Enid. "He really brought down the tone of the evening."

Jessica and Sam sat on opposite sides of the Wakefield kitchen table, their heads bent studiously over their homework assignments. Underneath the table, Jessica's shoeless foot rubbed against Sam's.

"Cut it out, Jess," ordered Sam with absolutely no conviction. "I'm trying to concentrate on the Prussian War."

"What am I doing?" asked Jessica innocently. "I'm sitting here, doing my math, minding my own business . . ."

Sam gave her a look. "You never mind your own business, Jessica Wakefield, and you know it."

"Not when I'm needed, I don't," Jessica answered. "There are times when a girl just has to do what a girl has to do."

Sam gave her another look. "This sounds like you're taking charge of the life of Lila Fowler," he guessed.

Jessica sighed. "I only wish I could. But there doesn't seem to be anything I can do. I even tried talking to Jennifer Mitchell, John's old girlfriend, today, but she couldn't help either."

Sam put down his book. "Lila's still having a hard time at school?" he asked with concern.

Jessica nodded, explaining how things had gotten worse instead of better.

Sam shook his head. "So Lila's being punished because she's attractive and she's gone out with a few boys?"

"Exactly," said Jessica. A serious look came into her eyes. "It's made me realize that if this had happened to me instead of Lila, people would have treated me exactly the same."

Sam trapped her foot with his own. "Not in front of me they wouldn't," he said quickly. "They wouldn't dare."

"Oh, no?" Jessica teased. "And what would you do about it?"

"Don't forget," he said, reaching for her hand. "I'm Han Solo. I'm tough."

"And I'm Princess Leia." She grabbed his wrist. "I'm tough, too."

Sam leaned across the table to give her a kiss. "Not with Han Solo you're not. With Han Solo you're an angel."

They pulled apart just as Mrs. Wakefield came into the kitchen. The two of them started to giggle.

Mrs. Wakefield glanced over at them as she reached into the cabinet for glasses. "Your father and I have that video you wanted to see, if you and Sam still want to watch it with us," she said with a mischievous smile.

Jessica pushed Sam's hand away and straightened out her textbook. "We can't, Mom," she said earnestly. "I have to finish this assignment tonight."

Mrs. Wakefield nodded. "Oh, I understand," she said. "I could hear how hard you two were working from the living room."

Sam grinned, pushing back his hair. "You know how amusing quadratic equations can be, Mrs. Wakefield. Especially when Jessica's doing them."

Jessica blushed. Not only had her mother noticed that she and Sam were back to their old, affectionate selves, she seemed to approve.

Mrs. Wakefield poured out two glasses of juice and put them on a tray with a bowl of popcorn. "Oh, I know," she said, nodding her head. "Jessica's always had a way with quadratic equations."

"She sure does," said Sam as Jessica trapped his ankle between her feet.

Lila was trying to get interested in the situation comedy she was watching on television, but though it was a show she usually enjoyed, that night there was nothing about it that struck her as even remotely funny. She was relieved when the doorbell rang. "I'll get it, Eva!" she called to the housekeeper, thinking that it was probably Jessica.

In fact, she had been so sure that the person on the other side of the door would be Jessica that it took her a few seconds of staring blankly at the pretty but unfamiliar face in front of her before she registered that it wasn't.

"Hello," said the girl with a shy smile. "My name's Susan Wyler. I know you don't know me, but I've seen you around school."

Lila nodded, feeling totally bewildered. She recognized Susan as one of the trendier and most popular sophomores. She wasn't just exceptionally pretty, she was the sort of girl boys turned to stare after as she walked down the street. The question was, what was she doing here?

Suddenly aware that Susan was waiting for her to say something, Lila nodded. "Is there something I can do for you?" she asked.

Susan looked a little uncomfortable. "Well," she said hesitatingly, "it's just that . . ." Her voice trailed off as she fiddled with the car keys she was still holding. She took a deep breath and started again. "Look, Lila," she said, rushing on. "I'm really sorry to bother you, but a person would have to be in Tucson not to know what happened at your party Saturday night."

Lila could feel the blood drain from her face. Had this girl come all the way over here to tell her that she must be lying about John because he was such a nice guy?

Seeing Lila blanch, Susan reached out instinctively and touched her hand. "I'm really sorry to just turn up like this, but I have to talk to you,

134

Lila. I have something to tell you that I know you'll want to hear."

It couldn't have taken Susan Wyler more than ten minutes to tell Lila her story, but by the time she was done Lila felt as though years had passed. Susan Wyler had gone out with John Pfeifer after he broke up with Jennifer and before he had asked Lila out. She had driven out to the beach for a moonlight stroll with John, and she had had to fight him off. The only thing that had saved her was the sudden arrival of another couple. Terrified, Susan had gotten a ride back to Sweet Valley with them.

"I don't believe this!" breathed Lila when Susan was done. "I didn't even know John dated anyone else after Jennifer."

Susan leaned back on the sofa with a look of relief. "That's because you're the first person I've told," she admitted. "And anyway," she said with a sour smile, "you couldn't really call it dating. It was more like an invasion." She nervously folded and unfolded her hands. "I was so scared afterward—I thought it must have been my fault somehow. You must know—" She blushed. "Well, you *do* know. I've been watching how some people have been treating you since you confronted John, and I just had to come and say something to you."

Lila moved over to the sofa. "I can't tell you what a relief it is to talk to you," she said. "It's been so awful ... sometimes I think maybe I made the whole thing up, you know?"

Susan nodded. "I know, believe me. But I've been feeling really guilty because I didn't have the nerve to speak up the way you did. If I had, maybe all this wouldn't have happened to you."

Lila made a face. "I didn't exactly speak up, if you want to know the truth. I just sort of blurted it out."

"It doesn't matter," said Susan. "All that matters is that you did." She sat up a little straighter and looked Lila in the eyes. "Anyway, I came tonight to tell you that I'm not afraid anymore. I'm willing to speak up, too. I can't stand by and see people ostracize you the way they're doing. Not when I know the truth."

"I don't believe this!" said Lila, allowing herself the first real smile she had had in days. "I guess it really is true that it's always darkest before the dawn!"

"You bet it is," said Susan.

Lila looked at her shrewdly. "I take it you already have a plan," she said.

A smile lit up Susan's pretty face. "If I confront John alone, he'll only deny it and ignore me the way he denied and ignored you, right?"

Lila nodded. "Right."

"But if we go together—if John sees that we're united and strong—then he'll have to realize that he's been beaten." Her expression became serious. "If we can get him to go for help, then we'll have won," Susan said. "I think that's what our goal has to be."

Lila made a face. "I was hoping our goal was going to be to hang him from the flagpole at Sweet Valley High," she said. "But I guess getting him into counseling will have to do."

# Ten

"You seem to be in a good mood today," Eva commented as she set Lila's breakfast down in front of her on Wednesday morning.

Lila gulped down her juice. "I am," she said truthfully. "I'm feeling great." *What a difference a day makes,* she thought to herself. The day before, she got ready for school with all the enthusiasm of someone getting ready to go to prison. She didn't care what she wore. She had no appetite. She took the long way and drove slowly. Not today, however. This morning she had dressed in one of her nicest outfits, and although she was hungry, she was also so anxious to get the day started that she could barely sit still.

"Don't eat so fast," ordered Eva, noticing the unladylike way in which Lila was stuffing French toast into her mouth. "You'll get indigestion."

Lila smiled to herself. What was a little indigestion compared to finally triumphing over John Pfeifer and his lies?

"Oh, Eva," Lila groaned, but with a smile. "Stop worrying, will you? I'm fine." Pushing back her chair, she got to her feet. "Anyway, I've got to get going or I'll be late."

Eva glanced at the kitchen clock. "Late?" she repeated. "What are you talking about? You have plenty of time."

"No, I don't," said Lila with a shake of her head. "I have a ... a meeting before school starts." She threw her napkin on the table and picked up her books. "It's very important."

Eva frowned. "It better be, if you're rushing off without finishing your meal."

"Oh, it is," Lila assured her as she headed toward the garage. "It's *very* important."

Lila's hand touched the note in her pocket as she started up the Triumph. She and Susan had composed it last night. Short and to the point, it asked John to meet Lila at the Dairi Burger that evening. *I can't go on like this*, Lila and Susan had written. *We really need to talk.* The girls were sure that John, being the kind of guy he was, would think Lila wanted to strike a deal so that people would stop treating her so badly. Now all Lila had to do was get to school a little early and slip it into his locker.

"After what I've been through, I never thought I'd be looking forward to sending a note to John Pfeifer," Lila said out loud as she backed the

139

sports car into the street. "But this is going to be a real pleasure."

Jessica buckled up her seat belt on Wednesday morning, only half awake. "I don't believe this," she mumbled as her sister backed the Jeep out of the driveway and onto Calico Drive. "It's barely dawn and you're making me go to school." She pointed above them to the pale white crescent in the blue California sky. "Look!" she protested. "The moon's still up."

Elizabeth grimaced, her eyes on the road ahead. "Jessica, please. You knew I had to get to school early this morning. I have to finish off my piece for *The Oracle*. The paper goes to bed this afternoon. If it's that big a deal you should have taken a lift with Mom."

Jessica gave her sister a look. "You know I don't like to ride with Mom if I can help it. She always lectures me about safe driving." She leaned against the window as though trying to get back to sleep. "Now I not only have dark circles under my eyes, but I have nothing to do for at least half an hour."

"You can always come to the *Oracle* office with me if you really have nothing to do," said Elizabeth as they headed toward the high school. "Penny might be able to use an extra hand."

Jessica scowled. "Not if there's any chance that I'll run into the creep."

"Well, speak of the devil," said Elizabeth as they entered the school parking lot.

John Pfeifer was just locking the door of his car. He waved as they passed him.

"Don't you dare wave back," ordered Jessica as Elizabeth nodded in John's direction. She pretended to shudder. "I don't know how you can stand to talk to him. He makes me want to gag."

Elizabeth gave her a wary glance. "Don't get me wrong, Jess," she said, "but in this country a man is innocent until proven guilty. I try to keep my distance from John, but I can't cut him dead completely."

"So I see," said Jessica coolly, watching John as he crossed the lot toward them. "But I can. There's Lila's car. I'm going to see if I can find her." She jumped out of the Jeep and slammed the door shut as John came up behind them.

"Morning, Jessica," he said with a smile.

Jessica tossed back her hair, lifted her head, and stalked by him without so much as a glance.

"Lila Fowler, what are you doing?"

Lila jumped. She had been so sure there was no one around as she slipped the note into John's locker that she nearly screamed out loud. She swung around, afraid to discover who it was who had caught her in the act, only to find herself face to face with her best friend. "Jessica!" Lila breathed a sigh of relief. "What are *you* doing here?"

That suspicious look that Lila knew only too well came into Jessica's eyes. "I asked you first," she said. "What are you doing at John Pfeifer's locker?" She put her hands on her hips in a way that always reminded Lila of Mr. Cooper, the principal. "You're not backing down, are you?"

Terrified that John might come along at any

moment and catch them, Lila grabbed hold of Jessica's arm and started pulling her down the hall. "Of course I'm not," she hissed as she steered her into another corridor. "It's a little late now for me to back down."

"And it's a little early for you to be hanging out in the hall," said Jessica. She came to a sudden stop. "Come on, Lila," she insisted, "what were you doing there?"

Lila looked around nervously. Satisfied that there was no one within earshot—and no one who even remotely resembled John Pfeifer—she turned to Jessica with an earnest expression on her face. "Promise you won't tell anyone?" she asked. "I don't want this to get back to John, or everything will be ruined."

Jessica made an incredulous face. "Me?" she asked in a heavy whisper. "Me, leak a secret? I can't believe I'm hearing this!"

Lila squeezed her arm. "Promise!"

"OK, OK," said Jessica, shaking herself free. "I promise. Now what's going on?"

As quickly as she could, Lila explained about her unexpected visit from Susan Wyler the night before, and of their plan to talk to John together and make him go for help.

Jessica couldn't disguise her delight. "That's wonderful!" she said, giving Lila a quick hug. "You see! I told you you'd done the right thing in speaking out!"

Lila nodded. "I know," she said, her voice serious. "I guess Susan is right. If she'd said something, it might never have happened to me." She smiled wryly. "Still, I don't think I've ever felt as alone as I have in the last week."

Jessica linked her arm through Lila's. "Well, you're not alone anymore," she assured her. "Just tell me what time you want your supporters to turn up at the Dairi Burger tonight."

"Are you sure Lila won't mind if I come along tonight?" asked Elizabeth as Jessica pulled into the Wakefields' driveway. "I'd like her to know that I've been behind her in this, even if I have had to be polite to John."

"Of course she won't mind," said Jessica. "She said she wanted some moral support." Jessica knew that she had promised Lila she wouldn't tell anybody about Susan and Lila's plan to face up to John that night, but she reasoned that when Lila said "nobody" she didn't actually mean *Elizabeth*. After all, Elizabeth wasn't *nobody*—she was Jessica's twin. "I was even thinking of asking Sam to come. I figured that might look more normal, if we just happened to be there having a soda."

Elizabeth climbed down from the Jeep. "That's a great idea!" she said enthusiastically. "Why don't I ask Todd to come, too? That would look even more normal."

Jessica gave her sister a mischievous grin. "Why, Elizabeth Wakefield," she said with a wink. "I do believe you're learning to be sneaky."

Elizabeth smiled at Jessica over her shoulder as she led the way into the house. "It must be genetic," she said with a laugh.

"What if he doesn't come?" asked Susan as she followed Lila into the Dairi Burger that night.

Lila looked around, frowning. "If he doesn't come, he'll be the only person in Sweet Valley who isn't here," she said, indicating the crowded tables. Way at the back, tucked into a corner, she noticed Jessica, Elizabeth, Sam, and Todd. The boys had their backs to her, but the twins both acknowledged her with the slightest of nods. For all she had told Jessica to keep her big mouth shut, she had to admit that she was relieved to see them. If there was one thing this whole awful experience was teaching her, she decided, it was the value of friends.

"What do you think's going on?" asked Susan as she and Lila found a table at the side. "This place seems pretty busy for a Wednesday night."

Lila picked up a menu. "From the looks of the crowd, I bet there was a volleyball game tonight," she said, wishing she had thought about that before she suggested meeting here.

Susan laughed edgily. "So much for our private little meeting," she said.

Lila gave her a sympathetic smile. "Are you as nervous as I am?" she asked.

"More," said Susan, making a face. "Maybe this wasn't such a good idea, after all. I mean, it never occurred to me that it would be this busy."

"Well, it's too late now," said Lila with a sigh. She nodded toward the front, where John and a crowd of boys, most of them members of the volleyball team, were jostling their way through the door.

Both Lila and Susan studied their menus with intense interest as John and the volleyball players took their seats at a large center table.

"What do you think we should do?" whispered Susan.

Part of Lila thought that they should order a soda, drink it, and go. But another part, the part that realized that silence didn't solve problems or make them go away, knew that there was only one answer to Susan's question. "I think we should do what we came here to do," she said, quietly but firmly. "The sooner the better," she added, pushing back her chair.

In Lila's experience, a group of hungry boys who had just played a hard and fast volleyball game were usually hard to distract from burgers and french fries. But not these boys. As soon as she appeared next to John the entire table looked up, smirking and nudging John with their elbows. John raised an eyebrow. "Well, if it isn't the princess herself," he said. "Don't tell me you've finally decided to apologize to me for defaming my good name."

The other boys found this incredibly amusing. *Remember who you are*, Lila told herself. *Don't let these little boys intimidate you. You vacation in Eu-*

*rope and they spend all their time running around the gym tossing a ball.* She cleared her throat. "John," she said, relieved to discover that years of being who she was had given her enough poise and control to sound normal even though her palms were sweating. "John, I asked you to meet me here because I want to talk to you."

John leaned back in his chair. "Sure," he said breezily. "Talk away."

"I mean privately," said Lila, feeling her confidence rising in direct proportion to John's arrogance. "I don't think you'll want the whole team to hear what I have to say."

John gestured toward the other boys. "I have no secrets from my friends." He gave her a meaningful wink. "Unlike some people."

Lila smiled. John assumed that he had beaten her because he had brazened out her accusation. He probably thought she wanted to throw herself on his mercy, that she was going to lie and give him the apology he wanted. Her smile became a little brighter. *Well, you're wrong,* she said to herself. *You are very, very wrong.*

Lila stood up straight. "All right, Mr. I-Have-Nothing-to-Hide," she said, "I just wanted to tell you that I discovered something last night that I think you should know about."

John made a mock-worried face at the table. "What?" he asked. "That you've changed your mind again?"

Lila talked over the snickers. "No, that I have something in common with Susan Wyler." She saw a flicker of worry cross John's eyes. "You remember Susan Wyler, John," she continued in her sweetest voice. "Susan Wyler is the other girl who had the misfortune of going out with you recently."

John looked around at his friends. "I don't know what she's talking about," he said, laughing to cover his nervousness.

"Oh, yes, you do, John," said Susan, suddenly coming up behind Lila. "You know exactly what we're talking about."

Lila bit back a smile as she saw the other boys giving one another confused and uncomfortable looks. The boy sitting beside John, a guy named Dean, nudged him. "What's going on here, Pfeifer?" he demanded. "Susan's my kid sister's best friend, you know. She's practically part of my family."

John shook Dean's hand from his arm. "Nothing's going on," he assured him, unable to keep the nervousness out of his voice. "The two of them think they're funny, that's all."

"Oh, sure, John," said Susan. "We think *you're* real funny, too. First you try to attack me, and then you try to attack Lila." She moved closer to the table, a new urgency in her tone. "Can't you see you have a problem, John? Can't you see that you should be trying to get help, not trying to act like nothing happened?"

An uneasy murmur went around the table.

"Susan and I are very worried about you, John," said Lila. "We think that you should get some professional help." She turned to the boy sitting across from John, who was beginning to edge his chair away. "Don't you think that someone who can't go on a date with a girl without trying to attack her should seek professional help?" she asked.

Dean stood up. "Yeah," he said. "Yeah I *do* think he should."

John tried to laugh. "Oh, come on, Dean. You don't believe—"

"Susan Wyler doesn't lie," he said sharply. "And neither does Lila Fowler, from what I can see." He shoved his chair in so roughly the table jerked. "Which leaves *you*, doesn't it, John?" Without another word he strode from the restaurant.

John looked around as the other boys began to move away. "You're not listening to these two, are you?" he asked. "Can't you see they're making this up?"

"Really?" asked Lila. "Why would we do that, John?" She turned to Susan. "Susan and I didn't even know each other before last night."

"That's right," said Susan. "I only went to Lila because I heard about what happened at her party." Her voice shook with emotion. "And I realized then that if I had spoken up before, when you did the same thing to me, it might have never happened to her."

John looked around in dismay as the last few players pushed back their chairs and slipped away. "Hey, where are you guys going?" he

148

asked. "We have to stick together. We can't let a couple of girls push us around."

A tall, blond senior put his hands on the back of John's chair as he walked past. "Maybe you'd better stop pushing them around, little man," he said quietly. "Maybe you should seek some professional help before some professional help seeks you."

Lila felt a hand placed gently on her own shoulder. She looked around to see Jessica standing behind her and Susan, and Elizabeth, Todd, and Sam behind her. "Come on, you two," said Jessica, in a voice that carried clearly across the restaurant. "Everybody else is getting as far away from John as they can. It's time *we* all got out of here."

Walking out the door with the others, Lila couldn't resist the urge to look back at John. He was standing at the empty table with a dazed expression on his face.

"Hey, you guys," Lila called to the others. "Wait for me!"

Jessica was in a good mood as she and Lila entered the Valley Mall on Friday afternoon. Not only had her parents agreed to let her buy something special to wear when Prince Arthur arrived in Sweet Valley in two weeks, but being out with Lila again made the past two weeks seem like a bad dream. She gave a little skip as they passed the fountain on their way to Bibi's, one of their favorite clothes stores. "I can't believe it!" she cried. "It seems like ages since we've gone shopping together."

Lila smiled. "It has been ages." She gave Jessica a look. "I don't mind admitting that there was a time there when I thought I might never shop again."

"Lila!" Jessica pretended to be horrified. "How can you say something like that? Don't you know that dozens of boutique owners depend on you!"

Lila laughed, but then her expression became serious. "You can joke, Jessica Wakefield," she said, a hint of her old smugness coming into her voice. "But it just so happens that there are real people who depend on me."

"You mean, besides the credit card companies?" teased Jessica.

"I mean other girls," said Lila as they entered Bibi's. "I've become something of a role model at school, you know." Jessica hid her smile behind a sea-gray silk shirt. "You mean Susan Wyler?" she asked.

"Not just her," Lila said, fingering a velvet skirt. "Do you remember the girl who came to my costume party with John? The one who was dressed as a rabbit? Well, she came up to me in the hall today to thank me for what I did!" Lila smiled over the dress rack at Jessica, obviously pleased with herself. "She said she felt that every girl at Sweet Valley owed me a debt of gratitude."

"Maybe they'll name a sandwich after you in the cafeteria," Jessica teased, but there was no malice in her joking. The simple truth was that she was relieved to see Lila getting back to her old conceited self.

Lila grinned back. "I think a dessert would be much more likely," she said, joining in on the joke. "Something rich and unhealthy."

Jessica scrutinized a dark pink blouse. "What about the counseling?" she asked gently. "When do you start that?" Amy had finally persuaded Lila that she should seek some professional help herself.

"Monday." Lila pulled a purple velvet sheath from the rack. "I just hope I don't run into John while I'm there," she said, her face clouding for a moment. "I think it's great that Barry and the other boys convinced John to go to Project Youth, but I really don't want to see him."

"I don't know if *convinced* is the right word," said Jessica. "I think threatened with being hauled up in front of Mr. Cooper is more accurate."

"Whatever," Lila said. "The important thing is that I want to get over this as quickly as I can." She held the dress up in front of her.

Jessica had to suppress a smile. The sheath was definitely one of the hottest things in the store, and Lila was going to look terrific in it. "Oh, I think you're getting over it just fine," she said.

When Jessica got home that afternoon, she found Elizabeth sitting at the kitchen table, a pile of opened letters on the table in front of her. As Jessica dumped her packages, the letters fluttered and scattered.

"Are those what I think they are?" Jessica asked. An impish grin crept up on her face.

"If you mean are these Arthur's letters, then yes, they are what you think they are," Elizabeth answered as she gathered the pages and neatly stacked them.

"It looks like there are a lot more than three, Liz. What's going on?" Jessica sat down and rested her chin on her folded arms.

Elizabeth smiled. "Nothing's going on. I just wanted to reread his letters from the past four years. You know, to sort of reacquaint myself with him, to . . ."

"To see if you're in love with him?"

"What! Not you, too!" Elizabeth exclaimed. "Jess, we've been through all of this before. I am not in love with Prince Arthur, and he's not in love with me. and that's that."

Jessica stood up and grabbed her package. "Hmm. We'll see," she said as she turned to leave. But as she reached the door of the kitchen she turned back.

"You know," she added, "if you're really not interested in Arthur, I just may know someone who *is*."

Will Prince Arthur find himself a princess in Sweet Valley? Find out in Sweet Valley High #91, **IN LOVE WITH A PRINCE**.

# The most exciting stories ever in Sweet Valley history...

FRANCINE PASCAL'S

**SWEET VALLEY** *Saga*

☐ **THE WAKEFIELDS OF SWEET VALLEY**
Sweet Valley Saga #1
$3.99/$4.99 in Canada                    29278-1
Following the lives, loves and adventures of five
generations of young women who were Elizabeth and
Jessica's ancestors, The Wakefields of Sweet Valley
begins in 1860 when Alice Larson, a 16-year-old
Swedish girl, sails to America.

☐ **THE WAKEFIELD LEGACY: The Untold Story**
Sweet Valley Saga #2
$3.99/$4.99 In Canada                    29794-5
Chronicling the lives of Jessica and Elizabeth's
father's ancestors, The Wakefield Legacy begins with
Lord Theodore who crosses the Atlantic and falls in
love with Alice Larson.

**Bantam Books, Dept SVH10, 2451 South Wolf Road,
Des PLaines, IL 60018**

Please send me the items I have checked above.  I am enclosing $＿＿＿
(please add $2.50 to cover postage and handling).  Send check or money
order, no cash or C.O.D's please.

Mr/Mrs＿＿＿＿＿＿＿＿＿＿＿＿＿＿＿＿＿＿＿＿＿＿＿＿＿＿＿＿

Address＿＿＿＿＿＿＿＿＿＿＿＿＿＿＿＿＿＿＿＿＿＿＿＿＿＿＿

City/State＿＿＿＿＿＿＿＿＿＿＿＿＿＿＿＿＿＿Zip＿＿＿＿＿＿

Please allow four to six weeks for delivery.

Prices and availability subject to change without notice.        SVH10 6/92

# SWEET VALLEY HIGH®

### Celebrate the Seasons
### with SWEET VALLEY HIGH
### Super Editions

You've been a SWEET VALLEY HIGH fan all along®— hanging out with Jessica and Elizabeth and their friends at Sweet Valley High. And now the SWEET VALLEY HIGH *Super Editions* give you more of what you like best—more romance—more excitement—more real-life adventure! Whether you're bicycling up the California Coast in PERFECT SUMMER, dancing at the Sweet Valley Christmas Ball in SPECIAL CHRISTMAS, touring the South of France in SPRING BREAK, catching the rays in a MALIBU SUMMER, or skiing the snowy slopes in WINTER CARNIVAL—you know you're exactly where you want to be—with the gang from SWEET VALLEY HIGH.

## SWEET VALLEY HIGH SUPER EDITIONS

☐ **PERFECT SUMMER**
25072-8/$3.50

☐ **MALIBU SUMMER**
26050-2/$3.50

☐ **SPRING BREAK**
25537-1/$3.50

☐ **WINTER CARNIVAL**
26159-2/$2.95

☐ **SPECIAL CHRISTMAS**
25377-8/$3.50

☐ **SPRING FEVER**
26420-6/$3.50

---

**Bantam Books, Dept. SVS2, 2451 S. Wolf Road, Des Plaines, IL 60018**

Please send me the items I have checked above. I am enclosing $_____ (please add $2.50 to cover postage and handling). Send check or money order, no cash or C.O.D.s please.

Mr/Ms _____

Address _____

City/State _____ Zip _____

SVS2—1/92

Please allow four to six weeks for delivery.
Prices and availability subject to change without notice.